The Boston Embalming Girls

by

Lee René

The Boston Embalming Girls

Cover Art by *The Wild Rose Press, Inc.*

The Wild Rose Press, Inc.
PO Box 708
Adams Basin, NY 14410-0708
Visit us at www.thewildrosepress.com

Publishing History
First Edition, 2024
Trade Paperback ISBN 978-1-5092-5573-3
Digital ISBN 978-1-5092-5574-0

Published in the United States of America

Dedication

This novel has gone through several incarnations, and it is my pleasure to finally share it with an audience. Thank you to Tim Cogshell for suggesting that I write The Boston Embalming Girls and to Linda Hollander for editing the early editions of the manuscript, opening up the city of Boston to me, and suggesting source material. Thanks to my parents and to my late friends who are forever in my heart.

Chapter 1

The Boston and Providence Railroad Station at Park Place is a wonder of the age, eight hundred and fifty feet of brick ornamented with gilded spires and stone arches buttressed by hand-chiseled caryatid columns.

Boston Illustrated, 1878

The acrid scent of burnt coal permeated the icy air, and I bundled my cloak against the chill. A thin coat of oily dust covered every inch of the train platform, and I could not risk fouling my cloak by sitting on the sooty plank bench. Still, the filth of my surroundings did not temper my excitement. My pulse raced with the expectation of my new life in Boston.

The spicy aroma of the young man's Bay Rum cut through the scent of scorched carbon. I turned and caught the eye of a young fellow in a greatcoat and silk cravat. He tipped his top hat, his teeth glinting sharp and white in the autumn light. Despite his fine clothes, the youthful dandy was as repellant as a villain in a dime novel.

He took a step in my direction, and I averted my face, praying he would not attempt to start a conversation. As luck would have it, a slender girl in a

1

black woolen gown reached me first. She extended her gloved hand, a broad smile warming her face. "Excuse me. Are you Miss Thorpe, Miss Delight Thorpe? Madame Thorpe said to search for a black-haired girl with blue eyes. She sent me to escort you to Bram House."

I gave thanks when my admirer glared at the interloper and walked away.

The young lady appeared no older than my own seventeen years, but instead of girlish plaits or curls, she had swept up her locks in a fashionable Titus cut. A deep brown fringe framed her face. Her spectacles did not conceal intelligent eyes that seemed to take in everything.

I acknowledged her with a handshake. "I'm Delight Thorpe."

As she pumped my hand, her lips spread into a broad grin. "And I'm Abigail Allgood, but you must call me Abby."

Her smile never left her face. "We should be on our way. Madame Thorpe is waiting."

Abby grabbed my battered carpetbag, and we marched from the platform.

Once we were inside the Boston and Providence Station, the beauty of the place overwhelmed me. The guidebook's description had not prepared me for the profusion of alabaster, Italian marble, and crystal chandeliers inside. We strolled past a grand dining room, stopping long enough to peer through its lead-glass windows and admire the potted palms and elegant gilded fixtures.

Four young men of commerce milling about the entrance turned in our direction. The fellows wore identical black waistcoats and silk ascots with gaudy stickpins. They all sported mutton-chop sideburns and reeked of cologne. The young men tipped their hats at our approach and grinned like feral dogs.

My new friend took my arm. "Be wary, Delight. Whoremongers stalking comely girls lurk in every corner of Boston."

We left the station and found rows of carriages, coupes, landaus, and broughams lined up in wait. I pointed to a hansom cab. "Shall we take that one?"

She dismissed my suggestion with a shake of her head. "Why waste money on a hack when we can take a streetcar instead?"

Given my new circumstances, it paid to be prudent with money. We mounted a horse-drawn trolley packed with commuters. Straw covered the floors, and riders packed the vehicle like tea biscuits in a tin. Three boys engaged in a loud and smelly flatulence contest, but we ignored them and concentrated on the beauty of the city instead.

Boston had reemerged from the great conflagration of 1872 like a phoenix reborn. Now, instead of burned-out husks, grand buildings dominated every block. Despite the city's magnificence, refuse and mounds of horse dung fouled the streets. Overworked dray horses clip-clopped through the city and left droppings as if silently protesting their labor.

Abby took my hand in hers. "Madame Thorpe told me of your losses. I am so sorry."

Although it took effort, I mustered a smile. "Thank you, Abby. Now with Uncle Ephraim's untimely death, I'm afraid poor Ziba has her grief. I hope I can be of comfort to her."

My companion's lips quivered, and I knew she might break into sobs. I had already shed my every tear and did not join her.

She squeezed my hand. "Yes, your uncle's unfortunate accident took us all by surprise. That horrible fall from the stairs broke his neck like a twig. Now, your poor aunt, a widow of twenty, is alone in the world. My dear parents died from diphtheria three years ago, so I understand her loss…and your loss too."

Her voice caught once again, yet she continued speaking. "Madame Thorpe mentioned the deaths of your friends when influenza ravaged your village. Would you, could you allow the young ladies who assist your aunt to take their place? We're virtuous girls, walking a straight path. At present, the three of us are a jolly trio, my cousins, the Duffy twins, Clara and Patsy, and me. We live together in a boarding house. My cousins are grand young girls, but it's just not the same as having a proper family. I used to pray that we'd find another young lady to join our circle, and now we have. Thank the Lord, our trio will now be a quartet."

Abby spoke in a conspiratorial whisper. "By the way, my cousins wear identical frocks, but one can easily tell them apart. Why they bother to dress the same, I'll never know."

She clasped her hands together. "Oh, the times we'll have together."

I did not contradict her, but how could strangers take the place of those I knew from childhood, girls who would forever be in my heart?

She tilted her head in my direction, her eyes misting. Although it may have been of little comfort, I placed my hand on hers. "It seems we are kindred spirits."

4

The trolley lurched forward and then moved at a maddeningly lackadaisical pace, halting long enough to allow a group of schoolchildren to pass. Gargantuan public buildings lined the north side of the street. Worn banners from the recent presidential battle reminded me of another election that barred my sex from voting. I turned my gaze to the opposite street but immediately wished I had not.

The rouged and mustachioed body of a young man, stylishly garbed in a waistcoat and striped trousers, sat in a parlor chair in the picture window of the McCarthy and Hyde Undertaking Parlor. A sign on an artist's easel announced *Mr. Clayton Webster, Embalmed Three Months Ago.* An embalmer had crossed his right leg over the left, and his hands lay folded in his lap.

The sight chilled me to the core of my being as if a block of ice had crawled up my spine. I gasped at the display. "I've read the Paris Morgue displays pickled corpses. Do the good people of Boston take pleasure from such monstrosities?"

She patted my hand, a placid smile on her face. "Don't be concerned. McCarthy and Hyde's work is so slipshod they force their vulgar displays on the citizenry. They aren't the artists we are."

'We are?' Before I could ask her meaning, the trolley lunged forward once ágain. I exorcised the macabre sight of the embalmed corpse from my mind and changed the subject. "I understand Ziba has taken over her father's business."

Abby chuckled. "Yes, and both she and your late uncle made Dr. Bram's enterprise a success. Despite her youth, Madame Thorpe's clients come from the finest houses of Boston to seek out her skill."

5

The jolly, red-faced conductor at the front of the conveyance shouted out, "Next stop, Patriot Street, then Browning Court and the famed Garden of Dreams."

Abby gave my hand another squeeze. "We're almost there, Delight, Browning Court, and the Garden."

"Garden?" I could barely contain my joy. "Ziba never wrote about a garden. What a marvelous surprise."

I did not have time to enjoy this revelation because the streetcar made another abrupt turn, nearly sending us both to the floor.

The trolley lumbered down Patriot Street, a boulevard covered with silvery Belgian pavers and bordered by maple trees and quaint shops. The conductor stopped the trolley and pointed. "There's Browning Court, a hop, skip, and a jump to the Garden of Dreams."

For once, joyful tears rolled down my cheeks. Hearth and home awaited me around the corner. The stench of death and the cries of the dying would soon be remnants of the past. My throat caught when I thought of meeting Ziba again.

We had seen each other once, two years prior, when she and my uncle visited our village during their honeymoon. At the time, I wondered why such a vibrant girl, barely eighteen, would wed a handsome but dour fellow of thirty-five. Then, a month ago, just before Mama's death, we received a telegram informing us of my uncle's passing.

Abby and I disembarked leaving the warmth of the trolley for the chill of the street. I pulled my cloak tighter about my shoulders against the cold.

When I saw the street sign reading, "Browning Court," I mouthed a prayer of thanks. Without warning, three fair-haired children, two boys, followed by a tiny girl, dashed past, chasing a large wooden hoop spiraling over the pewter-colored pavement. The boys wore black velvet suits with lace collars. Breton sailor hats topped the golden ringlets that bounced about their shoulders. Abby sneered at the tykes.

"Beware of those dreadful children, Delight. They are not innocent tots. Devilish spirits lurk beneath their cherubic appearances."

The hoop bounced over the paving bricks, and the boys giggled, undoubtedly gleeful over some prank. The girl had the same angelic features as her siblings and wore an elaborate winter ensemble of black velvet and fur. She appeared to be around four and ran as fast as her chubby legs allowed.

The two hellions glanced back at her, laughing as they darted toward the only domicile on the court. My heart almost flew from my chest the moment I first caught sight of a whimsical affair with seven pointed gables decorated with elaborate rococo trusses. Stone tracery and crawling vines concealed the walls, and arched windows stared out onto the street like great hooded eyes, Bram House, my new home.

Without warning the hoop rolled up to the gate, and the children began to chant, "Worms' meat and maggot pie, worms' meat and maggot pie."

A tall woman garbed in a crisp black uniform swept the porch. At the sight of the children, she threw down her broom and rushed to the edge of the stairs. The woman yelled at the tiny rowdies, her voice booming with anger. "Stay away from here, you little buggers. Have you no respect for the dead?"

"Respect for the dead?" I turned to Abby. "What is she speaking about?"

7

My companion seemed perplexed at my question. "Why the family business, of course."

The serving woman picked up the broom and returned to her task, mumbling loud enough for us to hear her words. "Those little bastards need the strap."

Abby tittered at the woman's words and squeezed my hand. "You'll soon get used to strong language. You're in Boston now, my dear."

The imps continued their devilish cry as they rushed off.

A gentleman of color turned over the flowerbeds. His pitchfork cut into the hard earth. He appeared oblivious to the children's shenanigans. The hoop bounced past the open gate, and the little girl yelped with joy. The three children rushed down the street, screaming like banshees.

This charming place, the only residence on Browning Court, adjoined a massive wrought iron gate. I peered through the bars at verdant lawns, Grecian statuary, and masses of marble grave markers. Grave markers? I looked deeper. My eyes had not misled me.

The Garden of Dreams sprawled before me, a giant cemetery.

In the blink of an eye, my new home lost all its charm. A gravedigger working on the grounds stopped his labors. He removed his bowler, revealing a head of matted brown hair. He appeared in his early thirties, his sinewy body covered with sweat. The fellow possessed ordinary looks except for green eyes as cold as a reptile. The gravedigger stared at me in a most disquieting way.

"Now who might you be, Little Missy?"

His insolence stunned me, and I did not speak. What possessed the fellow to address me in such a familiar manner?

The blackguard smirked and spoke again. "Cat got your tongue, Missy? Are you lost or something? Maybe I can help you find your way."

A furious Abby stepped in front of me. "Riley, this young lady is Madame Thorpe's niece. If you have any sense left in your gin-soaked head, you'll leave her alone."

He hissed at my new friend. "Keep your nose out of it, Miss High and Mighty."

I responded to the cad, my anger getting the best of me. "Sir, I'm not your 'Missy.' I must ask you to refrain from speaking to me."

Abby took my arm, and we marched off. The gravedigger kept pace with us and muttered salacious comments from the other side of the fence. "You don't have to be afraid of me, girlie. I'd never hurt a sweet little piece like you."

Our steps quickened. We rushed past the entrance of the cemetery and only paused to focus on a massive cast iron sculpture of the Furies. The three deities hovered above the colossal front gate as if protecting the necropolis and its inhabitants. How I wished they had dispatched the despicable fellow.

"You're a proud beauty, Missy."

I turned to face the scoundrel and nearly collapsed from the stench of spirits on his breath. He laughed at my reaction. "Such a pretty thing, but too full of yourself to give a poor Mick like me the time of day, ain't you? But maybe I got something you'd want."

Abby gasped in shock. "Riley, I always knew you were a cur."

The gravedigger snorted. "Who asked you, girlie?"

If I had been carrying an umbrella, I would have rapped him soundly on the head. "Your manner is offensive, sir. You have nothing I want or will ever want."

Thankfully, the gardener stepped between us, brandishing his pitchfork. "Riley, you heard the young ladies. Now, skedaddle, or I'll stick this fork up your rump!"

Mr. Riley puffed up his chest like a black adder. "You wanna start, lemon drop?"

The gentleman threw down the pitchfork and took the stance as if prepared to engage in fisticuffs. "Back to work with you, or I'll beat you to a pulp and tell the young mistress you're soused again. This time, you'll get the sack for sure."

Abby handed me my carpetbag. "Delight dear, I better leave before I get into an argument with the drunken oaf."

She signaled to the groundskeeper. "Mr. Greer, Miss Thorpe is here." She scowled at Riley and then rushed off.

Riley glared at me and the gardener, and then staggered back through the cemetery gate, grumbling under his breath.

I gazed into the gentleman's face. His features marked him as Cape Verdean or a mulatto from the West Indies.

"Please, don't mind him, miss. Gin makes him act crazy."

I took a deep breath. "I'm fine. I've encountered ruffians before. Sir, I believe Miss Allgood called you Mr. Greer."

He shook his head in the affirmative. "Yes, miss, the

name is Greer, Prince Greer."

"Well, Mr. Greer, Miss Allgood said you could direct me. I fear I'm lost. I'm searching for Mrs. Thorpe, Mrs. Ziba Thorpe. She resides at 5 Browning Court."

The gentleman looked deep into my face. "Are you Miss Delight Thorpe?"

"Yes, I am."

He pointed to the house at the cemetery gate. "Then, you're at the right place. Bram House is over there."

I read the sign affixed to the wrought iron gate. When I saw the words engraved on the bronze placard, the zephyr returned and crawled up my spine.

5 BROWNING COURT
THE BRAM FAMILY MORTUARY
&
COLLEGE OF EMBALMING

Chapter 2

Bram House

Mortuary? My new home? No, it could not be.
"There must be a mistake, Mr. Greer."

He pointed to the charming residence. "There's no
mistake. The young mistress lives there, at 5 Browning
Court. Dr. Bram, her father, worked as an embalming
surgeon. Her mother, Madame Bram, embalmed the
dead as did your late uncle."

It took a moment to absorb his words. "Embalming
surgeon did you say?"

"Yes, miss."

"Oh. Perhaps it would be best to seek lodgings
elsewhere." I turned on my heel only to face Mr. Riley.
The villain stood at the cemetery gate, leering at me. I
spun around and marched back to a confused Mr. Greer.

"You seem distressed, Miss Thorpe?"

"Yes, I'm afraid I am. You see, I thought Ziba, uh,
Madame Thorpe, managed her late father's medical
practice."

He took my bag and gestured toward the house. "In
a way, she does. Madame Thorpe has continued her
father's work, the holy art of preparing the dead. We've
been waiting for you, miss. I worked for Dr. Bram, then
for your uncle before his passing, and now for Madame
Thorpe. The young lady has been anxious about your

arrival. Please follow me."

He opened the gate. What else could I do but walk behind him? Returning to Rachel's Pride was out of the question. I climbed the steps to the portico and yanked the bell pulley.

The portal opened, and the tall woman who had chastised the mischievous tykes stood in the doorway.

Mr. Greer beamed at the woman, a sparkle in his orbs, and a wide grin on his lips. His expression told me more than words could. "Miss Thorpe, may I present my wife, Bride Greer?"

A hint of a smile danced across her handsome face. "Please come in, miss. I would have recognized you anywhere. You favor the late Dr. Thorpe."

I nodded at the mention of my dead uncle, gulped down my fear, and crossed the threshold. "Thank you."

Like Mr. Greer, his wife was of mixed blood, but her golden skin and amber eyes differed from the Cape Verdeans I had known in my village.

Mrs. Greer winked at her husband before curtsying to me. We followed Mr. Greer into the foyer, a forest of Boston ferns, and hothouse flowers. Gaslight bathed the walls in a pale glow. The pungent scent of incense was overpowering, and I could not stop myself from retching.

She noted my distress. "Perhaps you'd like a cup of tea. Miss, forgive me, but you're as pale as a ghost."

Pale as a ghost? How apropos. I lapsed into a fit of nervous titters. "Please excuse me, but my father visited Boston when my uncle died. He never mentioned Madame Thorpe's occupation."

Mrs. Greer glanced at her husband. "I see. Coming here must be a shock. You should lie down."

"No thank you. If you please, I'd like to speak to

your mistress."

"Of course, miss. She's waiting for you."

A large ebony cat pranced into the foyer. The animal stared at me through caramel eyes then sat on her haunches to groom herself. When I knelt to pet her, the cat arched her back and hissed. Mrs. Greer shooed the creature away, flapping her apron like a bullfighter's cape. "Off with you, Hecuba."

The cat dashed away. Mrs. Greer laughed at her retreat. "The beast thinks she owns the place. Madame Thorpe named her after a witch, and it suits her."

She helped me with my cloak and bonnet, took my carpetbag from Mr. Greer, and then pointed to a set of French doors. "The mistress is making final preparations in the viewing salon. If you need me, miss, please call."

A plume of smoke from an incense urn curled up to the carved ceiling. Someone had lit the gas mantels. The gas jets illuminated the room thick with incense burning in small brass urns. I stepped into a battlefield of contrasting patterns and hues. Although it hardly seemed possible, the salon was even more vulgar than the foyer.

A man stood behind a portrait camera sitting on a tripod. Although a heavy black drape obscured his face, I noted his slender build.

He had positioned his camera in front of a carved oak box coffining the body of an elderly woman. One pale hand removed the lens cap, while the other pushed a trigger attached to a short cord. The deceased subject wore a simple gray silk gown, her gloved hands crossed over her bosom. Her wrinkled face appeared as if it had been carved from fine alabaster. Emerald-colored gaslight sconces tinted her skin pale green. A cap of French lace covered her white hair.

The photographer pulled his head from beneath the black drape. I could barely make out the contours of his face, but the dark-haired fellow appeared to be no older than eighteen. "This will make a lovely *carte de visit.* The family will be pleased."

The young man spoke in the genteel tones of a gentleman.

A blonde woman and another fellow walked over to the coffin and scrutinized the deceased. "My ladies did a splendid job, didn't they, Charles? How lifelike she seems in her peaceful slumber."

Her companion, a tall, fair-haired man, wore an elegant black frockcoat of the gentry. I could not make out his features, but he was clean-shaven, eschewing the heavy muttonchops some dandies wore.

"It is the longest slumber of all, my dear Ziba. Poor Mother Bicknell is finally at rest."

He spoke with a distinctive Brahmin accent, his youthful baritone, strong and resonant. "Father had to dissuade her family from using the services of McCarthy and Hyde."

Ziba's face reddened and exploded into rage. "I wouldn't let those belly punchers embalm a dog. Shanty Irish scum, they're no better than common stevedores from the docks."

I shuddered at the memory of the embalmed body I had glimpsed from the trolley. Ziba's companion placed a reassuring hand on her arm. "Now, now, Ziba, there's no need for rancor. No family of quality would allow those ruffians in their home."

The young man's words calmed her, and her mood lightened considerably. "You're right of course, Charles. They might be villains, but I'll forget them."

A lull in their conversation gave me leave to enter the room. I called out to my young aunt.

"Ziba!"

My beautiful aunt turned toward me. She wore a mourning gown styled in the new fashion, form-fitting ebony velvet without a bustle.

She rushed to embrace me. "My darling Delight, I thought you'd never arrive. Thank the Lord, my trials are at an end. Our merciful Father has delivered you from that place of misery. I should box your ears, you naughty girl, for making me wait so long."

I found myself engulfed by the potent fragrance of her lilac toilet water. "My sweet girl."

When she released me, I took in her appearance. She had arranged her flaxen blonde hair in a chignon with a fringe of ringlets that framed a face as delicate as a porcelain doll. However, with her rouged lips and cheeks, her face dusted with rice powder, she seemed more like a woman of the streets rather than a young widow. Then, I remembered her suffering and chided myself for my uncharitable thoughts. Perhaps all Boston women availed themselves of cosmetics.

Ziba took me by the wrist and pulled me over to the casket. When I balked, she giggled. "Don't be afraid of old Mother Bicknell. The poor dear is quite harmless now. You mustn't mind her, darling girl. Now, I have a special someone for you to meet, a friend of our family."

She looked up at the gentleman, a flirtatious *moue* on her rouged lips. After her loss, who could blame her for casual coquetry? "Charles, may I present my niece, Miss Delight Thorpe? Of course, she'll be more of a sister than a niece. Delight, this is Mr. Charles Reeves, but I insist you call him by his given name, for you'll soon be friends."

Mr. Reeves glanced up and extended his hand in welcome. "Miss Thorpe, I'm honored."

Ziba laughed as she made the introduction. "Don't be a stick in the mud, Charles. She's Delight, and you're Charles."

I will never forget the moment I first laid eyes on Charles Reeves. Mr. Reeves stood before me, well over six feet in height, as handsome as any actor who trod the boards. With his fair hair and inviting smile, his features were those of a prince. He was truly the most imposing gentleman I had ever seen, though to be honest, I had seen very few. The young man spoke in a voice so resonant that I imagined his timbre and diction would put Mr. Maurice Barrymore to shame. I took his hand in greeting, praying fervently that he would not notice my blushes.

Charles could not have been over twenty, yet he exuded a maturity beyond his years.

I steeled my shoulders. "Hello, Charles." His green eyes sparkled with a mischievous twinkle, and it took a Herculean effort for me not to avert my gaze.

The young man took note of my distress and squeezed my hand. "You must pardon me for staring, Delight, but I knew your late uncle. I see the Thorpe in your features."

He took in my scuffed boots. "Don't tell me you walked here from the rail station?"

I felt the warmth of a blush move up my face. "No, uh, Charles, I traveled by public conveyance with Miss Allgood. We had a grand adventure."

Ziba pouted like a fractious child. "Thank the Lord Abby accompanied you. With all the mashers in Boston, who knows what mischief you might have gotten into? You mustn't ever strike out alone. You're not in the country anymore, you naughty puppy."

The photographer called out to her. "Should I take another photograph, Madame Thorpe?"

"No, the family will be here soon, so there is no time. Come, Edgar, you must meet my Delight."

"Yes, of course, of course. Miss Thorpe, I—"

The boy named Edgar whipped his head around in my direction. His hair fell into dark curls that framed a delicate face. The paleness of his skin set off a pair of beautiful eyes, dark, lustrous, and sad. Edgar had the melancholy air of a poet about him. He stood motionless, staring at me. Despite his beauty, I found his gaze disquieting.

Charles came to my rescue and clasped the young man by the shoulder. "Eddie, the hour grows late. It's time for us to be off."

Edgar appeared to awaken from his reverie. "Yes, of course, Charles." He turned to the older boy but then focused his eyes back on me once again. I averted my face and fixed my attention on my harp and Mama's mandolin. The sight of my old friends cheered me to no end. Ziba had placed a splendid oak lyre stand next to my instrument.

She shut her fan and then pushed a parlor chair behind the harp. "Delight dear, your arrival is most timely. There'll be a viewing tonight, so I engaged a musician to play your harp. Unfortunately, the Silly Billy shrieked like a baby the moment he saw poor Mother Bicknell. Imagine a grown man wailing like a starving infant. Delight, would you, uh, help us? I took the liberty of having your exquisite instrument tuned. Harp music would set a lovely tone for the wake."

Charles pulled Ziba aside. "Ziba, I don't wish to intrude, but the poor girl has just arrived. Surely you can't expect her to perform tonight?"

She smiled at him through clenched teeth. "The family paid for music, Charles, and we shouldn't disappoint them, should we?"

He shrugged as if he realized the futility of arguing with her. "Very well, if you insist."

I found her request impossible. I had just arrived at a house of horrors, my stomach growled, and grime from the train covered every inch of my body. Ziba expected me to wake a corpse, the last straw to break the laden camel's back.

"But I'm filthy from my travels and haven't eaten supper yet. I can't play my harp with that poor creature in the casket in the room. I can't. I can't."

Ziba set her jaw and pinched my cheeks. "Ah, now your face has a lovely glow to it. You look quite fetching, and your lovely music will set such an elegant tone. We must be mindful of our clients, and Delight, remember, you are family."

She called out into the entryway. "Bride, Bride, where are you?"

The serving woman raced into the salon. Ziba flashed a bright smile. "Bride dear, please bring refreshments for Miss Thorpe, tea and sandwiches."

Ziba turned to me, a scowl on her face as she scrutinized my travel costume. "If only we could change your gown."

She looked at Charles, sulking like a child. "Don't blame me for the way she dresses. I offered to engage a proper seamstress, but she declined and said I'd been too generous already." Ziba's attention returned to me, and she had a bright smile on her face. "Dear girl, wait until you see the newest fashions. Boston is quite gay these days, and everyone is wearing narrow skirts. Small bustles are quite the mode for young ladies, but one still sees trains and large bustles on matrons. I've copies of the latest *Harper's Bazaar*. You must peruse the fashion plates."

Ziba's face fell once again. "Pooh, there's no time for you to change into something more appropriate. I guess that rag you're wearing will have to do."

Her remark cut me to the quick. "My gown may not be new, but before influenza took her, Mama and I refashioned it from her second-best frock. We even trimmed her best bonnet with tartan rosettes to match the dress."

Even Edgar rose to my defense. "I think she's enchanting."

Ziba dangled one of my hands before Charles. "These dreadful hands belong to a washerwoman, not a young lady of quality."

He grimaced at Ziba's words before turning back to me, a smile lighting up his handsome face. My heart raced, and I could have spent the rest of the evening gazing at him.

"My dear Ziba, leave her alone. I think Edgar would agree that Delight knows the value of hard work, unlike many young women in our society."

Edgar chimed in. "Yes, indeed, Charles."

Ziba spoke to Mrs. Greer through clenched teeth, though her annoyance as with Charles and Edgar. "Bride, please put the orange flower cream in Miss Thorpe's room and take care she uses it."

She turned toward me, an angelic smile gracing her face, her voice simpering. "Delight, when your late father visited Boston, he spoke with great pride about your skill at the harp. Make your beautiful music for us, please."

I fixed my gaze on Charles, silently entreating him to intercede. Perhaps he realized the futility because he didn't. Resigned to my fate, I plucked at the strings of my harp, played a bold glissando, and then started Brahms' *Magelone Romances.*

Ziba whispered to Charles. "I wager you won't see or hear anything like her at Hyde and McCarthy."

"Agreed, dear Ziba, agreed."

Charles's presence was calming, that is until I noticed Edgar standing off in a corner, his attention still focused on me. Perhaps I should have been flattered that such a handsome lad appeared interested, yet the intensity of his gaze disturbed me.

I moved from Brahms to *Ondina Oberthur's Conte de Fees,* and finally to J.S. Bach. My fingers plucked the strings, but I could not take my eyes off the corpse lying near me. I averted my face, but the casket remained in my periphery. Candlelight flickered across the dead woman's face.

Perhaps there had been a trick of the light, but I glimpsed a change in her position. The body seemed to move. The old woman's left shoulder had risen ever so slightly. I struggled to contain myself and wondered if the gas jets of the chandelier that hung above had cast shadows. Inch-by-inch, the cadaver appeared to be rising from the casket.

Another *glissando* and the woman's breast rose. I strummed the harp strings. Her shoulders ascended by a fraction of an inch then her upper torso levitated from the coffin, resurrected. I had no memory of specifics, but later Ziba said before I collapsed, I screamed loud enough to raise the dead.

Chapter 3

First Night

When I opened my eyes, I found myself upright in the chair, Edgar at my side and Ziba fanning me. Charles held a small glass filled with a brownish liquid to my lips.

"Please, drink the brandy."

I gulped the spirits down then found the taste so revolting that I coughed it up. Ziba twisted her fan with a nervous laugh. "Mother Bicknell wasn't alive. Mr. Greer must have been a tad careless when he placed her in the casket."

Charles's forehead furrowed, his brows knotted in concern. Then he smiled at me, and I thought I would swoon again, but not from horror. "Ziba, I told you Delight would need time to acclimate to life here."

She ignored his words and continued fanning me. "My poor Delight, the old woman couldn't walk erect and was bent nearly in half. Although the coffin was deep, we had to secure her body to lay her out. The cords must have come undone. Even death couldn't hold the old girl down."

I averted my face as Mr. Greer tied down the body for the second time.

The door pulley chimed. I yelped once again, almost jumping from my chair. Mrs. Greer rushed into the room and whispered into my young aunt's ear. Ziba peered toward the hallway and then back again at me, desperation written on her face.

"Drat, the first mourners have arrived. Delight, could you, would you—"

I found her audacity unbelievable. "Ziba, are you mad? I can't play in a room with that poor woman in her casket."

Charles appeared shocked by her suggestion and stepped away from the coffin. "My dear girl, please, you can't be serious. Delight has just arrived and needs to adjust to living here."

She ignored him, patted my cheek, and favored me with another dazzling smile. "But you must. Mother Bicknell is secure now, and her family did pay for music." Her smile turned into a reproachful pout.

"You're a Thorpe, aren't you? Delight dear, I need your help."

I realized pleading would be fruitless and began plucking at the harp strings. Ziba turned to Charles, her face triumphant.

Two hours later, I left the viewing salon barely able to place one foot in front of the other. I made my way into an elaborate circular room decorated in the same gaudy hues as the entryway. Twin settees nestled in jungles of potted palms set on either side of the carved staircase. Hecuba lay curled at the foot of the steps, purring. I took a tentative step toward her, my hand extended.

"Here puss, puss."

The cat arched her back again, hissing with such ferocity I bolted, and bumped into the young photographer.

"Please excuse me, Miss Thorpe."

He fixed his eyes on me, and I moved away to escape the intensity of his gaze.

"No, I should apologize since I backed into you."

He extended his hand, his eyes never leaving my face. "I'm afraid that we weren't properly introduced. My name is Edgar, Edgar Reeves, Charles's younger brother. Mr. Greer, the colored fellow, told me about the loss of your family. I'm so very sorry."

I searched his face for a fraternal resemblance, but I could not find one. Charles, a robust fellow, bristled with energy while Edgar had a delicate build, his skin so pale I knew the sun had never kissed it. He continued to gape at me and did not notice Mrs. Greer's entrance into the foyer.

The cat purred as she rubbed against her leg, but her feline show of affection did not take in the housekeeper. "Shoo, you vile creature or I'll turn you into a foot warmer." She glared at the young photographer. "Mr. Reeves, sir, it's late, and Miss Thorpe has had an evil long day. You should leave now."

He remained rooted to the floor. "Yes, of course. Good evening, Mrs. Greer. Good evening, Miss Thorpe."

I managed a smile and walked past the young man. "Good evening, Edgar."

Hecuba sashayed past us, her tail held high in the air. She sauntered up the staircase then turned back as if daring us to follow her. Bride and I ascended halfway when I heard a resonant baritone. "Good evening, Delight."

Charles stood at the foot of the stairs, a broad smile on his lips. Heat moved upward from my chest to my neck. My cheeks warmed with color, but I managed to speak. "Good evening, Charles."

I took another step, but something stopped me from ascending the rest of the way. Despite the cold, something hot enough to consume me burned into my back. When I turned and peered down the staircase, Charles stood at the landing. I prayed for Our Lord and Savior to still my heart—without my dying, of course.

I stopped at the second-floor threshold. "Mrs. Greer, I have a question. Do you embalm the dead here?"

She cackled then wrapped her shawl a bit tighter about her shoulders. "Mercy no, the holy work's done in the basement, and please call me Bride. You don't have nothing to be afraid of, miss, except for the chill. It's wicked cold in parts of the house, like a witch's teat. Considering the clientele, that's good, ain't it?"

I could not decide what was more disquieting, the icy air, the grotesque ruby and indigo wall coverings, or the grim portraits of generations of members of the Bram family. Gas jets concealed in the sconces gave the corridor a faint, phosphorescent glow. A door creaked open, and I jumped.

Bride steadied me then chuckled. "Don't be frightened, miss. There's something off about the place. Doors open and close at will. You'll like living here when you get used to it. There's a bathtub with running water and an indoor privy."

Bram House had an indoor privy? "Goodness, I've read about water closets but never thought I'd live in a home that had one."

She smirked and then opened the last door in the hallway. "Here's your room, miss."

I peeked inside before I gave a yelp of joy and

rushed in. Unlike the garish viewing parlor and entryway, the furnishings of my bedchamber were subdued and welcoming. A four-poster bed sat in welcome as did the mahogany wardrobe with a matching chest of drawers. Someone had placed my ditty box on an étagère and arranged my bisque doll, seashells, and scrimshaw. "I unpacked your things, miss, such as they are."

A splendid toilet set, complete with sea sponges and vinegar water, rested on a wooden stand next to a porcelain washbasin and a pitcher of steaming water. Bride pulled the top drawer of the bureau open. "Take a gander, miss. Madame filled the chest with new camisoles, split drawers, petticoats, and corsets, the best in Boston."

I found it impossible to stop my squeals of joy when I saw the underwear. "Goodness, these are so much finer than my own. The camisoles and petticoats must be silk. What luxury."

Bride handed me a pair of clean split drawers. "Fresh underwear for you, miss."

After my travels, I needed a wash. I pulled off my undergarments and stood before her sans petticoat. A marvelous scent wafted from a basket filled with bars of aromatic soap and perfumed the room.

"I've never smelled such a heavenly fragrance. Is the soap imported from the Continent?"

She chuckled, pulling back the coverlet. "Heavens no, miss. It's made right here in Boston, special for us, the best on earth, Dr. Bram's Funeral Soap."

I dropped the fragrant bar. *"Funeral soap*?"

A smirk danced across her lips. "To wash the dearly departed. If it makes the dead smell good, just think what it does for the living."

Despite my reluctance, I scrubbed away the grime of the journey with perfumed soap. Bride helped me into my clean underwear, pulled a night chemise over my head, and then draped a bed shawl over my shoulders.

"Madame Thorpe wants you to have the hands of a lady, miss."

"Dear Bride, I fear your work is cut out for you. I've stacked wood, cooked, scrubbed, and sewn since I could walk. My hands are like a stevedore's."

"Leave them to me, miss. I'll have them beautiful for when you play your music."

Bride tackled the redness with lemon, fine white sand, and borax powder. She massaged my hands with Orange Flower Crème just as Ziba had instructed. "You'll have beautiful hands in no time."

After she finished, Bride pointed to the rosewood wardrobe set against the wall. "You might want to explore what's in that wardrobe."

I could not stop myself from another enthusiastic whoop when I opened the wardrobe doors. Stylish ensembles, bodices, and skirts in the season's colors, dove gray, forest green, ebony, navy, and claret packed the wardrobe along with slippers of every hue.

"It won't matter if they don't fit, Bride. I'm a wizard with a needle and thread. I'll soon be a lady of fashion."

I pressed the maroon bodice to my bosom and twirled about the room. Bride had drawn the heavy drapery against the cold. As I sailed past, I pulled at a gold sash, opening it. The swathe of fabric had concealed a large window that afforded a view of a brick courtyard. Someone had tethered an elegant coupe drawn by a matched set of black geldings to the post near the carriage house. I had never seen such a fine vehicle.

"There's a splendid two-seater in the courtyard below."

Her tone cooled considerably when she replied. "It belongs to young Mr. Reeves. He's a real demon behind the reins, drives those horses as fierce as the devil."

What a bold fellow he was. "He's quite the most dashing gentleman I have ever seen."

She met my comment with stone silence. When I turned to face her, she averted her face. "Wouldn't know about such things, miss. I have a man of my own, and I don't have eyes for no others. My husband is the only colored embalmer in Boston or anywhere else I'll wager."

She removed the heating iron from under the mattress and then pulled back the heavy winter blankets and counterpane before banking the fire.

I twirled about the room, dancing my version of the Boston waltz. I was determined to put my grief at bay. Bride tittered at my antics.

"Dance away, miss. The young mistress will be so pleased that you liked the gowns. She bought all of them and the furniture too after Miss Elda Rice died of consumption."

Consumption? I stopped prancing about and placed the bodice back in the wardrobe.

Bride fluffed the pillows, clucking like a mother hen. "Now don't be worried, miss. Everything's been cleaned real good, new mattress and all. The Rice girl won't be needing her fine clothes, will she?"

I had to agree. "Yes, you're right. After all, I arrived in Boston in my dead mother's gown. Perhaps I'm fated to dress in the clothing of those dearly departed."

Bride picked up the tintype of a young girl holding a mandolin from the étagère and gazed from the image to me.

"What an elegant portrait. Is this you, miss?"

The image showed my mother dressed as a muse with a garland of flowers artfully arranged on her head.

"No, it was Mama on her seventeenth birthday. Yes, she was handsome, wasn't she?"

"You're her spit and image."

"Thank you. Everyone praised her beauty, but I'm afraid I'm a poor imitation."

She positioned my mother's portrait back on the étagère, tempting me to compare my comeliness to hers. A small mirror rested on the table, and my hand went to it. Instead, I turned away, chiding myself for vanity. No matter how hard I fought vanity, I still fell prey to it.

"Here is my father." I pulled an image of Papa in his dress uniform from the war.

Bride swooped up the image and then sighed before handing it back to me. "Now this is a man. Such a handsome fellow."

I caressed the frame and placed it next to Mama's image. "Everyone said Papa had been the most dashing chaplain in the Union Army."

I pulled out another, a beautiful dark-haired little boy. "This was my brother, Alfred Tennyson Thorpe. He died at five from the measles." I choked back a sob. "I have no photographs of my friends."

I had sworn to myself that I would not spill another tear, but although they welled in my eyes, I refused to let them fall. It was not fitting to weep in front of a stranger, so I changed the subject.

"Ziba has a brother, doesn't she? I believe his name

is Theodore." Although I had never met him, I vowed to be a second sister to the four-year-old tyke. "Is it possible to see Theodore tonight? In all the excitement, I forgot to ask about him."

Bride answered with a shake of her head. "No, miss. I'm afraid Master Teddy is already asleep."

"Teddy? You call him Teddy? How charming."

"You'll make the little fellow's acquaintance tomorrow."

She hesitated as if she wished to tell me something. I prayed she might tarry, but she took her leave instead.

"Well, miss, it's time for me to be off. Can't lollygag, and besides, you must be worn out from your travels. If you're afraid of the flush toilet, the chamber pot is under the bed. The slop basin is in the water closet, so empty it there. Prince and me stay over the carriage house, so I won't hear nothing if you ring."

I hated to see her leave, but I knew she must. "I'll lock the door after you, Bride."

"There's no lock, miss. Good night."

She closed the door, leaving me alone.

Chapter 4

The Light in the Garden

I sat alone in the chamber. The memory of my losses remained fresh, akin to a stab in the heart. My soul still bled, and I doubted the pain would ever disappear. My tears started the moment I slumped onto the bed. Would my travails never cease? Still, with the Lord's help, I would persevere. At that moment, I vowed to do anything Ziba asked. I might even embalm if I must, that is, once I get used to the idea. I was a very diligent worker.

I perused the room and fixed my eyes on a wooden stationery box that sat on the étagère's top shelf. When I opened it, I discovered a cache of fine linen paper scented with pressed violets, a gilt inkwell, blotter, embosser, and franking postage. The late Miss Rice had etched a message in the wood.

This is the property of Elda Rice, age 17, 10 Sutton Place.

I hoped Miss Rice would not mind my using her implements to write to my only friend in the world, my old schoolmarm, Charity Yates.

November 16th, 1880
The Good Hope Inn
Rachel's Pride, Massachusetts
Miss Charity Yates

Dearest Miss Yates,

It has only been a few hours, but I already pine for you and Rachel's Pride. I pray the suffering will soon be at an end and life will begin anew. Thank you once again for the vast sum of one hundred and thirty dollars you gave me when I left Rachel's Pride. I shall protect it and only use it if I need to.

Boston is a city of great wonders. The ladies garb themselves in the most stylish fashion, but one must question how they are able to maneuver their long trains. I fear there is madness in the air that makes men act in a most repellent manner.

Praise the Lord, my dear Ziba has welcomed me into her bosom and opened her fine home to me. Bram House is quite splendid. There are gaslights and an indoor privy. I have not used it as of yet, but I plan to one day soon.

I shall write regularly. Please give my regards to all those who are still with us. May you walk in the path of righteousness, my dear friend. We have both lost so much.

With great affection,

Your Delight

I prayed Our Heavenly Father would forgive my falsehood regarding my new life. The truth about Ziba's ghoulish commerce might alarm Miss Yates. I would not tell her.

The bed beckoned me. Papa's compass glittered from on the étagère. I reached for it and placed it under the pillow. Before I sought the comfort of slumber, I knelt and prayed for those buried in our local cemetery and the few who had survived. I might have stayed, but constant reminders of all those who had passed on pushed me away. Each morning, new burial mounds wreathed with tansy and bittersweet greeted me on my daily visits to the graveyard.

Sleep soon overtook me, and I dreamed of my village in summer when the fragrance of the sea mingled with the scent of partridgeberry, wild strawberries, and arbutus. The girls from my sewing circle wore summer gowns of white cotton and strolled through the birch grove behind the rectory. My dear father stood in the arbor arm in arm with Mama.

A shaft of moonlight lit the door to my room. The faint almost imperceptible sound of weeping awakened me from my glorious dream. At that moment, I knew that I no longer resided in Rachel's Pride and a dead woman rested in the parlor downstairs. When I heard metal upon metal, I remembered the door did not have a lock.

The portal opened, and gentle footsteps padded over to my bed. Someone had entered my room. Darkness prevented me from seeing the intruder, but I heard breathing, as though someone gasped for air, the same as my father's final breaths. When I pulled my hand back from the coverlet, something held it fast, stroking it with a touch as gentle as the fall of the first winter snow.

What had walked into my bedchamber? Perhaps if I screamed, it would disappear, but try as I might, I could not muster a peep. I shut my eyes and mouthed the Lord's Prayer.

Our Father which art in heaven, hallowed be thy name. Thy kingdom come, Thy will be done—

The breathing came to an abrupt halt, and the footsteps padded away from the bed. Someone or something threw the bedroom door open and then shut it, and I found myself alone again. I opened my eyes and sat up, gasping for air. A loud thud at my window punctured the silence. I rose from the bed and peeked through the draperies. The moon's silvery reflection, barely visible through the fog, illuminated the silhouette of a tree branch pushing against the glass. I sighed in relief and thanked the Lord. I could not have dealt with yet another apparition.

****

Minutes later, I dressed and made the bed. I placed the photos of my family and Papa's old compass in the carpetbag, grabbed my reticule, and opened the bedroom door. The corridor felt like a frigid void, but I crept down it and descended the great staircase. I found my way to the darkened kitchen and the door that I hoped would free me from this dreadful place. The portal opened, and I ran from the house.

The November fog sat in the air as viscous as chowder and made my way difficult. Had I wandered into another world? The screech of an owl reminded me I still walked the earth. A horse whickered, and I smelled the scent of hay and manure. I had reached the carriage house.

The heavy mist obscured my vision, but the waxing moon illuminated the courtyard. I saw an open gate and raced through it, moving as quickly as the fog allowed. My head thumped, my mind, a jumble. In my haste to escape, I had not thought about shelter for the remainder of the night.

I peered into the emptiness, saw a tall white figure, and yelled out into the distance. "Hello? Is someone there?"

When I approached the specter, I let out a breath of relief at a marble statue of a wailing woman. Through the fog, I could just make out the granite tomb adjoining the sculpted figure. A loon cried out somewhere in the graveyard, breaking the stillness and reminding me I had exchanged one fright for another.

I turned to walk back to the gate and then saw a glint of brightness ahead. I heard masculine voices, youthful ones. I was not alone. Someone strode from the darkness carrying a lantern, and I called out into the void. "Who are you? Please show yourself."

The intruder dropped the light with a thud and ran off into the night. I picked up the lantern, and its light revealed a newly disturbed grave. The pale body of an elderly man, hands crossed over his chest, lay next to an open burial pit. Resurrection men lurked somewhere in the Garden. I scurried toward the gate, screaming at the top of my lungs. An arm grabbed me, and a hand covered my mouth, silencing me.

Chapter 5

Rescue

If Fate had decided I should come to a violent end, I prayed my death would be swift. I took comfort from the gentle words of Psalm 91:1: *He that dwelleth in the secret place of the most high shall abide under the shadow of the Almighty.*

When my "murderer" spoke, I almost collapsed with relief. Charles pressed his face so close to mine that I smelled the scent of violet lozenges on his breath.

"Delight, I beg of you, don't scream again. What would Ziba say if your cries brought a constable here?"

Charles removed his hand from my mouth.

I turned and read the shock on his face.

"Delight, why are you out at this time of night?"

When I opened my mouth to answer, no sound came out.

Charles draped his greatcoat around my shoulders. "My poor girl, we must get you inside." He took my hand.

I followed him through the courtyard into Bram House's dark kitchen. Charles unlatched the door, and the lantern light spilled across the plank flooring. A pair of golden orbs stared out from the darkness like tiny beacons. Suddenly, the beast sprang forward and leaped to the top of a massive wood-burning stove. I shrieked

but then broke into nervous titters when I realized the identity of the monster, Hecuba, the cantankerous black cat.

Charles put his finger to his lips then picked her up and stroked her. "What a sweet puss you are." He placed the purring feline on the floor, grabbed a lamp then whispered, "Please follow me."

We crossed the sub-parlor threshold and entered an arctic void. "Charles, it's freezing here."

He nodded and pulled up the collar of his waistcoat. "Yes, it is, but I'm afraid there are many cold spots in Bram House."

Oddities of all sorts packed the room, animal skeletons, dusty medical volumes, and grotesque tintypes of deformed people. The place resembled a cabinet of curiosities. Charles took a place on the settee next to me and pointed to a stuffed owl glaring from its perch next to an elk's mounted head. "Taxidermy was one of Dr. Bram's passions."

Birds flew in a nonexistent sky while a bobcat in an eternal hunt tracked its prey through glass eyes. Prime specimens of Dr. Bram's obsession festooned the walls along with a copy of President Lincoln's death mask, an army rifle, and tintypes from the War of Rebellion.

Charles poured a glass of liquid amber from a decanter that sat on a side table adjoining a rolltop desk.

"I'm afraid Ziba has turned this place into a shrine to her father's memory."

My hands shook, and I could not hold the small snifter he offered me. He held it to my lips. "A nip of sherry should do the trick."

My memory of the brandy made me brush the sherry away, but Charles persevered. "My dear girl, I wouldn't

offer you sherry unless I thought it would calm you."

Although I found the taste strong, I savored the sweetness and sampled it again. Charles watched me intently without saying a word.

His head fell to one side. "Miss Thorpe, now would be an excellent time to explain what you were doing in the cemetery."

How could I begin my tale? Would he believe me once I told him what I had seen? "I beg of you, please don't think I'm ungrateful for Ziba's kindness. But, you see, I thought I'd be working in a doctor's practice, helping the unfortunates of Boston, not living in a house full of cadavers."

He offered me more sherry. I took a healthy gulp and found the flavor even more inviting.

"Charles, I'm not a sot, and I usually don't touch spirits except for a bit of elderberry wine at Christmas."

I saw a definite smile on his face. "So, I've amused you, have I? Feel free to laugh at my expense."

He placed his hand under my chin and tilted my head toward his. In the dim light, I saw his smile had disappeared. "Dear girl, I'm not laughing at you."

We sat without speaking while the liquor worked its magic and calmed my nerves. Unfortunately, an ornate English grandfather clock in the corner of the room chimed, and I nearly jumped off the settee. Charles placed a restraining hand on my arm and poured another sherry.

"No one would begrudge you just one more sip, my dear girl."

He slid the snifter toward me, and I pushed it away.

"Charles, perhaps another drink would be unwise."

"Please, just one more."

Ziba had assured me of Charles's sterling character, and I reconsidered. He brought the glass to my mouth once again. The liquor braced me, and I felt able to discuss my horrid story.

"Do you think that strong drink will take my mind off that poor man in the cemetery?"

He seemed perplexed by my words. "What poor man?"

The sherry warmed me, and I took another gulp. "Why the corpse of the old gentleman lying on the ground next to his coffin, of course. It's a vision I'll take to my grave. I almost stumbled over him. Surely you must have—"

Charles pulled the glass from my hand before I could take one more sip. From his confused expression, I doubt that he understood my words.

"Dear girl, I saw no one, no one at all. I was in the courtyard on the way to my carriage when I heard your scream. I didn't have a torch and could barely find you in the darkness. You still haven't told me what possessed you to stroll into the Garden at night?"

Did I dare voice what happened? I averted my head. "Charles, you'll think I'm mad."

He turned my chin toward him. "Tell me, what did you see?"

"Coward that I am, nothing, I saw absolutely nothing. Something, or someone, came into my room. I didn't see what or who because I never opened my eyes. The specter sobbed and touched me. I couldn't call out or stare it in the face. I'm ashamed to say, I ran away instead because I have no spine."

Charles placed his hand over mine. Such familiarity shocked me, but when I stared into his eyes and saw his concern, I did not protest. "Delight, you were justly frightened. No one could blame you for wanting to flee Bram House. If my brother weren't employed here, I would find it impossible to set foot in this accursed place."

"Accursed? Why do you say accursed?"

His concern changed to a sheepish grin. "Did I say accursed?"

I pulled my hand away. "Yes, I distinctly heard you say 'accursed.' Why is Bram House accursed?"

Charles sighed, his brow furrowed, and the corners of his mouth turned down. "What an ass I am. I've frightened you with a mere turn of a phrase, you, a poor innocent in an alien city, without funds—"

I did not think of myself as poor or innocent. "I have ten dollars from Ziba and another one hundred thirty dollars and forty-three cents from my friend, Miss Yates."

"A princely sum, my dear, but how long will it last? How can you live in this city without a position or references?"

I did not speak, but I am sure my eyes revealed all. I began sobbing more from frustration than fear. "I wish I had died in Rachel's Pride. Death would be better than this."

Charles appeared taken aback by my candor. "I see I've made matters worse yet again." He pulled a kerchief from his pocket and handed it to me.

"There is a solution, Delight. Please hear me out. You may have noticed Ziba has a strong will, yet on rare occasions, I have her ear. I'll speak to her about finding you other lodgings. However, I must ask you not to mention the unfortunate fellow in the cemetery. She'll think you've come unhinged."

He eased closer, whispering all the while. "Ziba is a young lady of a nervous temperament with the weight of the world on her shoulders. Considering her profession, I'm afraid she wouldn't be receptive to such information." He paused as if considering whether to continue. "I hate to speak of it, dear girl, but the graveyards of Boston are regularly plundered by medical students searching for specimens for dissection."

Charles released my hand before sighing in resignation. "There aren't enough cadavers to fill the need. It's a hideous situation, beyond our control. I'm ashamed to admit they are fellow students at Harvard and the authorities will do nothing. You see, a secret society of grave-robbing medical students has existed in Boston for well over a hundred years, but we never speak their name."

I inched toward him. "Can't you reason with the students? For the sake of their immortal souls, you must talk to them about their despicable practices."

He spoke in gentle tones with a touch of condescension, as if talking to a child. "Poor innocent Miss Thorpe, what a world you find yourself in. Those in the society have named themselves the Spunkers, a silly name for such dangerous young men. They are a secretive bunch and don't associate with those of us who study law."

Charles paused as if lost in thought. "They aren't content with dissecting the bodies of convicts, lunatics, and riffraff who've died on the docks. No one can reason with them because they're godless. Nothing deters them. They employ resurrectionists, men who steal corpses. They've managed to outwit traps on graves, even those rigged with explosives. It horrifies me, but as a man of faith, I pray the Creator will forgive them. Please, never utter their name to another. I beg you, swear to it."

"Very well, I swear."

He spoke in a whisper. "I have another request, one you might find far more difficult to agree to. Promise not to run away again. I couldn't rest for worrying about you roaming the city with no roof over your head."

After a moment, I extended my hand in comradeship. "Very well, I promise." He turned it over and kissed the palm.

I tried to remain composed, but it required great effort. Charles barely knew me, and besides, he could court any girl in Boston.

He released my hand and leaned back on the settee, an impish smile on his face that caused my heart to flutter. "Now, we must talk about you. Ziba tells me you play the pianoforte, and the mandolin, as well as the harp. How accomplished you are. I once tried the violin but wasn't very good. Eddie has mastered it. Bully for him."

He leaned over and gazed into my face. "My dear Delight, don't think me presumptuous, but I find you enchanting. Ziba told me your mother was French Canadian. Surely you inherited her coloring, but did she bless you with those delightful dimples as well?"

His words shocked me so much that I could not speak. Perhaps he took my silence as an invitation to greater intimacy. He moved close enough for me to count the golden flecks in his eyes. I doubted Mrs. Florence Hartley, the author of *The Ladies Book of Etiquette*, would approve. Charles brought his lips to my cheek and then moved them down toward my mouth.

Anyone seeing me jump off the settee would have assumed it caught fire. Charles's face reddened. He turned away, as embarrassed as I was. "You should return to your room, Delight. The sherry will help you sleep. I'll speak to Ziba about other accommodations. Please remember your promise. You won't run away again."

I nodded. "Yes, I promise. Good night."

Minutes later, I trudged up the stairwell, the lantern my only light. I had the peculiar sensation of someone boring into my back as if observing me. My eyes searched the circular foyer and found it empty.

Then, I caught a movement in the shadows—Charles.

Chapter 6

Teddy

The next morning, a knock at the door awakened me. My head throbbed, undoubtedly from the sherry, and I made a solemn vow to never touch liquor again. Heat rose to my cheeks when I remembered my encounter with Charles, his remark about my dimples, and finally, his attempt to kiss me. A young man of his breeding would never have done anything untoward, but in the future, I would make sure we were not alone together.

I fell back onto the pillow hoping for another few merciful minutes of slumber, but a child's voice roused me. "Hello."

Tiny feet padded up to my bed. I turned to my visitor and looked into the smiling face of a little boy. He was small for a four-year-old, with a broad face, slanted eyes, and a round head flattened at the back. His pale blond bob with a fringe across his forehead partially concealed tiny, low-set ears.

The child whispered into my ear, his thick tongue slurring his words. "Shush, she's sleepy." He motioned to something concealed beneath his jacket. "Surprise! Surprise! Surprise!"

The tyke giggled, pulled a dead wren from beneath his coat, and offered it to me. The door opened, and Bride bustled in carrying a pitcher of steaming water. She set it next to the commode and raced over to him.

"I searched all over for you, you little beggar. Imagine, scaring poor Bride half to death."

Bride took the bird from the child's hands and placed a towel over it. "Teddy, the nice lady don't want that dirty thing." She murmured under her breath, "I'll bury it outside, miss." He refused to budge when she took him by his arm. "Now, Teddy, you can't pester the lady, or she'll be peeved. What a contrary boy you are, Master Teddy."

Bride released the child, and he ran back to my bed, tittering like a little scamp. When she opened the draperies, the overcast sky tinted the room pale pewter. "Had a good sleep, did you, miss? I'll be serving breakfast downstairs in thirty minutes. Madame Thorpe wishes you to wear the wine-colored frock today."

Despite the chill in the room, I jumped from the bed and went to the window. When I peered down into the courtyard, I trembled less from the cold than from the view of the Garden through the glass.

I felt a tug on my nightgown and found Teddy gazing up at me, a sweet smile on his tiny face. I had once seen such a child in our village. Our apothecary called the boy a "Mongoloid idiot" and forecast he would have a short and painful life. The prediction proved true, and I prayed Teddy would not suffer the same fate. I turned to Bride. "Ziba didn't write Teddy was—"

Bride removed a claret-red skirt from the wardrobe. "A half-wit?"

Her words took me aback, especially with the child in the room. "Afflicted."

"Half-wit or afflicted, it ain't exactly something you shout from a church steeple, is it? Thanks be to God,

Madame Thorpe loves the boy as much as me and Prince do. She's been through it all right with her poor mother dying in childbirth and her father passing away. The mistress has her Teddy though. He's a good little lad, better than most around here."

I noted that Bride made no mention of my late uncle or his death.

Teddy giggled once again. Bride suddenly became quite gay and opened her arms to him. "Bride made cocoa for her Teddy."

He ran to her and attached himself to her skirt. Her amber eyes crinkled with warmth when she smiled down at the child. Bride moved to the door with Teddy entwined in the folds of her gown. She turned the knob, but I stopped her with my words. "Please stay a moment."

"What is it, miss?"

"Someone—someone entered my room last night. Could it have been you?"

Bride shook her head in confusion. "Me? No, miss. I told you, I live above the carriage house. I let out the last of the mourners then locked the place up tight as Dick's hatband. Only you, Teddy, and the mistress were in the house, miss. Madame Thorpe sleeps like the dead." She turned her attention to Teddy. "Teddy, was you in the nice lady's room last night?"

He shook his head no, Bride gave a chortle then turned the doorknob. "Don't know who your visitor was, miss, but it wasn't no ghost. They don't have hands."

I'm sure I blanched at the word "ghost." "A ghost, Bride? Why would you mention a ghost?"

She scrutinized the room as if concerned someone might be listening.

47

"Madame Thorpe and my husband don't like me talking about such things. In case you're wondering, my mam hailed from the old country and my father was a mulatto from Montserrat. My mother told me of souls stuck on this earthly plane. They don't harm, can't touch you because they don't have a body." She moved closer and whispered, "Ghosts are around us, miss. You see a shadow in the corner of a mirror or the pane of a window. You turn around, and you're alone. Other times, you feel the chill of winter when they're near."

Bride gave a curt smile before turning toward the door. "It's time for me to go, miss. I've got a breakfast to serve."

She had already crossed the threshold when I called out to her once again. "Before you leave, there's something else, Bride. I saw someone walking in the cemetery last night."

Her eyes went cold, and I remembered my promise to Charles not to mention the visitor in the burial ground. How I wished I had held my tongue.

"How could you see someone out there in the boneyard, miss? It was pea soup last night."

This time I censored my words. "I saw the light of a torch from the window and thought that someone was in the cemetery."

She seemed peeved. "Excuse me, miss, but they keep those graveyard gates chained at night. Nobody could get in there. I'd keep the spook in the cemetery to myself, or people will think you've gone daft."

Her words echoed Charles's warning from the previous night. Bride must have thought I had come unhinged. Thank the Lord I did not mention the corpse in the Garden.

She took a smiling Teddy by the hand, and they walked from the room.

"Good day, Miss Thorpe."

I began my preparations for the day, vowing not to recount my adventures in the Garden to anyone else.

Bride had set out a garnet-colored frock trimmed with satin ribbing, a small mesh bustle attached under the bodice's peplum. I opened the wardrobe and discovered matching walking boots and a bonnet adorned with wine-colored silk rosettes.

Once dressed, vain creature that I was, I gazed at my reflection in the wardrobe mirror. Despite my unfashionably dark coloring, many considered me handsome. Luckily, the horrible experiences of late did not show on my face, which still had the roundness of a child's.

I started my first full day in Bram House after the terrors of the previous night and my imagined ghostly encounter. When I turned to leave, I glimpsed something out of the corner of my eye. I whirled back, only to see my own reflection. Bride's words affected me more than I thought. I steeled myself for whatever lay ahead.

****

The stairwell was even more imposing in the light of day. Three smiling girls garbed in black bombazine, one of them Abby, stood in wait. When I reached the landing, Abby rushed over to me and took my hand. "Dearest Delight, allow me to introduce you to your newest chums. First, Miss Clara Duffy."

Clara greeted me with an embrace and a giggle. "Oh Delight, I'm positively thrilled to make your acquaintance and am elated that you've joined our jolly group."

Abby took the arm of the other twin and pulled her toward me. "And this is Patsy."

Patsy curtsied. "Pleased to meet you, miss."

From a distance, the Duffy girls seemed identical with the same moon faces, dark red hair braided into thick plaits, freckles, and pug noses. When I moved closer, I noted Clara appeared to be an inch taller, with bright azure eyes that twinkled when she spoke. "Delight, I've dreamed of the day when another girl would join us. It's splendid, simply splendid. I can't wait to show you all the delights of Boston."

Patsy, the shorter of the twins, possessed lively gray eyes. "Yes, Clara is right. Boston is splendid indeed."

She spoke with a slight lisp that must have stopped her from chatting away like her sister. Clara took my arm. "We'll have wonderful adventures together, dear Delight. There are so many things to do here if you are of a cultural bent, museums, temperance lectures, and the theater. Oh, the fun we shall have."

Bride entered and pointed to a large room adjoining the foyer. "Breakfast is waiting, ladies." She acknowledged me with a wry smile. "That frock suits you, miss. The young mistress picked well."

I stepped into the dining room with a substantial breakfast of porridge, sausage and bacon pie, black pudding, and buttered toast spread across a massive table. Abby, Clara, and Patsy had already filled their plates with food and ate with gusto. Ziba waved me over to the table. "Come, Delight, join us. Bride is a wondrously skilled cook, the best in Boston."

The girls grunted in agreement then Clara spoke, her mouth half full with meat pie. "Yes, Delight, you must join us. Mrs. Greer's food is simply splendid, the best

I've ever eaten."

Ziba chortled in agreement. "Every nabob in Boston has tried to spirit our Bride away, but she won't leave me. I wager you never tasted such fine vittles in Rachel's Pride."

I joined them at a ponderous table with legs carved with images of roaring lions. Teddy had crawled beneath it and played with Hecuba.

Of all the Bram House grotesqueries, the dining room was the most outlandish. Heavy gilt-edged furniture packed the room, and gaudy silk covered the walls. A monstrous sideboard carved with symbols of the hunt, hounds, game birds, elk, and fish, dominated the room.

Between bites of food, Ziba waxed poetic about the frightful piece of furniture. "My dear mother became enamored with the sideboards in the great houses of the city and had to have one. By lucky chance, Charles's father, Dr. Reeves, had refurbished his home. Can you believe it, he gave us that beautiful Fourdinois along with the dining table and chairs. I wonder, how could he bear to part with such treasures?"

The girls chimed in agreement between slurps of tea and porridge. Abby scrutinized the garish chamber, an admiring smile on her face. "I sometimes question if heaven is as beautiful as this room."

My jaw must have dropped on the table. I had yet to meet Dr. Reeves, but he must have been overjoyed at ridding himself of these dreadful pieces. I kept my thoughts to myself and finished my porridge.

Ziba pouted across the table. "Delight, why must you be so stern?"

I attempted a smile, one that must have been quite

weak. "I need a bit of time for me to acclimate myself to the wonders of the big city."

She patted my hand. "Of course you do, but take heart, you'll become a Bostonian and will soon learn a profitable trade."

The twins tittered in agreement. Abby nodded, her lips spread in a huge grin. "Embalming is the rage now, and with two fine cemeteries nearby and another in Cambridge, business is booming."

Clara took a piece of buttered toast. "Oh yes, Abby tells the absolute truth. Embalming is quite in vogue. Marvelous, isn't it? We're always busy and will need more help."

Patsy lisped, "Yes, we shall." She turned to Ziba, a blush on her cheek. "We have Delight, but please make your next student a young man, Madame Thorpe."

The girls giggled away. Ziba dabbed at her rouged lips, leaving a trail of rose-colored pomade on her napkin. "My father knew embalming would be a golden opportunity. He never regretted being an undertaker, and with time, neither shall you, my darling Delight. I'll introduce you to the holy art after breakfast."

I'm sure my expression betrayed me. "So soon?"

Patsy lisped out a reply. "There's no time like the present, dear girl."

The others snickered in agreement.

Ziba took a bite of her toast and spoke between chews. "By the way, Bride told me you had a visitor in your room last night. Is that so?"

The girls turned their eyes toward me. I sputtered a reply. "Well, uh, I—" But before I could say another word, Ziba answered her question. "Whimsy, pure whimsy, a nightmare. My advice is not to dwell on it."

Bride entered the room carrying a fresh pot of tea. Thankfully, she had not mentioned the light in the Garden of Dreams. I acknowledged her with a nod. I would guard confidential matters more carefully in the future. At present, I was concerned with searching for proof of the cadaver in the cemetery, if only to convince myself of my sanity.

Ziba examined my plate and frowned. "Pooh, you've barely touched your food. Oh well, the girls will finish everything, but please know that it won't do. I won't have you starve yourself. As for that glum face, I'll tell a joke, that's what I'll do."

"My darling girl, I love tomfoolery." She spoke in a conspiratorial whisper. "I know it's naughty, but I have a marvelous collection of *Lord Fartman's Flatulent Foxhounds* and *Lady Cecily's Bloomers*." The tittering began. "Girls, I have a joke to share, a very clean one. What is the difference between two mermaids and spring and summer? The former are two daughters...the latter are two sea sons."

The girls broke out in peals of laughter, which encouraged Ziba even more.

Clara spoke first. "Tell another joke, Madame Thorpe. They always give us such pleasure."

"Very well." Ziba went into deep reflection and then chortled to herself. "Bride, I think you'll enjoy this one. It's cracking good. One night, two men were walking through the cemetery and heard a tap-tap, tapping coming from the shadows. They trembled with fear and discovered an old fellow chipping away at one of the headstones with a hammer. 'My goodness,' said one of them after catching his breath, 'we thought you were a ghost! What are you doing in the cemetery at this hour?'

The old man glared at them and grumbled, 'Those fools misspelled my name!'"

Bride joined Ziba and the girls in their deluge of laughter. I attempted to find humor in the joke, but try as I might, I could not. Ziba glared at me but then remembered herself and flashed a bright smile. "Old Sobersides are you?"

My attempts at telling jokes always failed, and my already grave personality had worsened over the past weeks. "I'm of a serious disposition, Ziba. Try as I might, I'm not good with humor."

"Well, you will have to get used to our monkeyshines. There's a lot of mirth in this house."

The girls and Bride giggled in agreement. I sat at the table like a bump on a log.

Chapter 7

The Garden

After breakfast, I begged to take Teddy to the Garden. "Please, Ziba. It's not healthy for a small child to be locked in this house all the long day."

Every bit of cheer left her face. "I won't have my little brother gaped at like a monkey in the zoo."

Thankfully, Bride chimed in. "Mistress, let her take our little lad to the boneyard. We'll dress him warm and give him extra cod liver oil against the chill. No one will bother him there."

Ziba hesitated for a moment. "All right, but don't tarry. You must acquaint yourself with our work."

Although the idea of watching an embalming did not thrill me, I attempted a smile. "Of course, Ziba."

Half an hour later, the kitchen door opened. Teddy flew out of Bram House like a canary from a gilded cage. He ran from the circular courtyard to a pathway, an obscure portal to the Garden. I raced after him and captured the child. "I have you, Teddy!" We entered the cemetery hand in hand.

According to my guidebook, Bostonians called the Abbott Browning Memorial Garden, "The Garden of Dreams," and considered it more beautiful than Mt. Auburn in Cambridge. Although the grounds had lost most of their emerald bounty, I marveled at serpentine walking paths, waterfalls, and lagoons. Unfortunately, the profusion of tombstones and a hearse in the distance reminded me we were strolling in a city of the dead.

As Teddy darted among the graves, I walked toward the statue of the wailing woman and examined the area near the gate. The grounds seemed untouched with no evidence of an open grave. I had once read resurrection men, professional grave robbers, could steal without leaving a speck of evidence. After what I had seen, I did not doubt it. From Charles's reaction, I surmised the grave robbers belonged to the Spunkers Club. He had even turned pale when he mentioned their silly moniker. Body snatching remained on my mind as I walked through the graveyard.

We passed a granite-and-marble Egyptian mausoleum surrounded by a moat. A stone bridge traversed the water and led to a wrought iron gate engraved with the name BRAM.

"Good day, Missy."

Riley leaned against a marble sarcophagus, leering.

"You're cunning handsome in that frock, Miss Delight."

The detestable man laughed when I took Teddy's arm and sped away. As I rushed toward Bram House, I wondered how he had learned my name.

****

The two little boys with the golden curls raced past the Bram House gate, in mad pursuit of a brightly colored kite propelled by a chilly November wind. They bounded down Browning Court leaving a trail of screams. "Bones for the boneyard, bones for the boneyard."

The little girl dashed after them but stopped dead in

her tracks when she spied Teddy. She stared at him for a long moment then bolted, giggling as she ran off.

The clang of the trolley reminded me of the letter that sat in my pocket. Public vehicles carried postal boxes, so Teddy and I rushed to the streetcar just in time to post my missive.

When we returned to Bram House, I placed my forefinger to my lips and whispered, "Teddy, we must be as quiet as mice."

We snuck into the foyer like two thieves. I averted my head when we passed the viewing parlor, praying I wouldn't see what rested there. Teddy, however, had other ideas. He pulled his hand from mine and darted into the room.

A small boy, his China blue eyes opened wide, sat on a tufted parlor chair in front of a white casket. He was dressed in a sailor suit, and his long curls, as black as the night sky, spilled over his shoulders. Teddy rushed up to the child and embraced him. I followed him and held out my hand to the little fellow.

"Hello, darling boy. My name is Delight, and this is Teddy. What's your name?"

The lad didn't stir, not even when Teddy kissed his cheek.

I took a step toward him. "Please tell us your name, sweetheart."

The beautiful tyke remained motionless. I took note of the brightness of the room and the portrait camera posed in front of the child. A familiar chill traveled up my spine as I drew nearer. Someone had painted bright azure-colored irises on the boy's closed lids.

I inched away from the small corpse, one small step at a time. Without warning, I felt warm breath on my neck, gasped, and then turned to face Edgar. He stood behind me, his dark hair rumpled, his eyes burning in a face even paler than on the previous night.

"I didn't mean to startle you. The child died two days ago. His family had no photographs of him, so I offered my services. I often paint eyes on the lids of dead children before I photograph them. It comforts the parents to have an image of their children looking as they did when alive."

Teddy wrapped his arms around the small corpse and kissed it again. Edgar snickered at the child, his laughter brittle and mirthless. Working in a mortuary had taken a toll on the poor fellow. "Please forgive us, Mr. Reeves, but we must be on our way. Teddy, come with me."

Edgar seized my arm before I left the room. I wrenched it from his grasp. "Mr. Reeves, let me go."

He colored slightly. "I beg you, please, call me Edgar, as you did last night."

I would have called him Abraham Lincoln to escape from his grasp. "Yes, of course, Edgar or would you prefer I call you Eddie, as your brother does?"

His body stiffened, and he took a step away from me. "No. My given name is Edgar."

For the first time, I noticed that Edgar walked with a pronounced limp and wore a built-up boot on his afflicted foot. He followed my gaze, and I saw the agony trapped in his eyes. "Now you see why I work for embalmers. Please don't pity me."

I shook my head. "Pity you? I don't pity you. Men who lost limbs during the War of Rebellion maneuver the streets of Massachusetts every day. Edgar, your limp doesn't matter a whit to me."

He smiled, the color came to his wan face, and once again, I could not deny the beauty of his features. Ziba entered the viewing parlor before he could utter another word. Teddy sped to her, his tiny arms outstretched. She pulled her brother close and then glowered at Edgar.

"Mr. Reeves, our clients don't pay you good money to fritter away your time. Please finish your work."

"Yes, of course, Mrs. Thorpe."

Edgar limped back to the tiny corpse. Ziba turned to me, her smile dazzling. "My darling girl, I think now would be an opportune time to introduce you to the holy art and my students. They await you."

I nodded to Edgar and followed Ziba to the stairway where a different trio of girls, day workers armed with brooms, brushes, and cleaning rags, stood at attention. Bride put them through their paces, dispatching them with the precision of a duty sergeant.

"Dust and sweep the upper floors, turn the beds, and empty the chamber pots. After that, everyone to the parlors and, in the name of Jesus, don't none of you get spooked by what's lying in those caskets. There'll be two viewings this afternoon and two days hence, a dinner, so get on with it."

The three serving girls curtsied Ziba. Bride pointed to the trio. "They're my cousins, miss. All of 'em came over from Ireland last year." She gave me a proud smirk. "They know English."

They all shared the same ginger-colored hair and freckles, but two of the girls had disfigurements. One had a harelip, another, crossed eyes. Bride pointed to the smallest of the trio, a comely girl of about fourteen.

"She doesn't speak, Miss Thorpe. The poor child lost her voice three years ago after a fever, but her hearing's good, and she can write a bit."

I watched as they made their way up the stairs. Surely, their defects prevented their finding positions in Boston's grand mansions. They appeared eager to work even if it meant laboring among the dead. Despite their afflictions, they had the same jolly demeanors as the embalming girls. The two older girls chattered away in a patois of English and Gaelic while the younger remained silent.

Ziba took my arm and led me to the stairs. "We perform the holy work in the basement." She chattered on as we descended the staircase. "Can you believe it, everyone in Boston is talking about the medium, Margaret Fox and her séances? They say she summons the spirits of the dead. Pooh, such poppycock. How can anyone believe in such garbage?"

I had heard of the spiritualist, Margaret Fox. Many called her a fraud, but I thought differently. My parents believed in Spiritualism and raised me to trust that God bestowed the gifts of communing with the dead to a select few. Still, the new Hades I would soon enter concerned me more than Miss Fox did.

By the time we reached the last step, girlish titters ruptured the quiet. Ziba could not contain her elation. "Oh my dear Delight, I'm thrilled you'll finally see our work."

Mr. Greer waited at the foot of the stairs. His smile didn't comfort me. "Good morning, miss."

Ziba urged me into the room. "Father transformed the basement kitchen and servants' quarters into a chamber where he perfected the holy arts."

Instead of the stench of rotting flesh, embalmers' soap and chemicals mingled with a whiff of excrement from the relaxed bowels of the newly dead. Embalming supplies, bottles of *Dr. Bram's Egyptian Embalming Fluid*, boxes of *Dr. Roulon's Wax Eye Caps and Mouth Closers,* and bars of *Madame Thorpe's Funeral Soap* piled in pine cupboards. Coffins of every shape and size flanked the north wall, and a storage unit dominated the south wall. A human skeleton, a reminder of the eventual fate of us all, dangled from a harness near the stairwell.

Ziba patted the skeleton's head as if it were a pet. "We call him Lazarus, but I'm afraid he won't be rising from the dead soon."

She turned to her giggling charges. "Ladies, a new day is upon us. Society once considered embalming the profession of surgeons but no longer. More importantly, despite the garbage those ninnies who publish *The Casket* and *Embalmers' Monthly* write, embalming is an endeavor where women are welcome. Families beg undertakers to let women embalm their mothers, sisters, and daughters, but I've heard embalmers lie and say there are no women morticians with my own ears. We've proven them wrong, haven't we?"

The room broke in applause. Ziba tossed her head back and gave a hearty laugh. "We're young, free, and embarking on a new venture together."

She pushed me forward, and the embalming girls greeted me with broad smiles. I noticed they all wore black leather aprons. "Delight is only observing today, but who knows what the future will bring?"

Clara applauded with great enthusiasm. "Splendid, splendid, Madame Thorpe. Patsy and I hoped a young man would join our ranks, but Delight is even better."

The room pulsed with anticipation, perhaps because of the presence of a new member of the embalming sisterhood. The girls were an agreeable bunch, but I did not want to join their ranks. Still, I responded with the sunniest expression I could muster and spoke a few words. "Perhaps my aunt told you I came from a small town where the village doctor embalmed. I know a little about your work. Why do you embalm?"

Ziba paced in place, a grin affixed to her lips. "A capital question. The War of the Rebellion created the need. The army once packed dead soldiers in charcoal and sent them home in cast-iron caskets, but the war changed all that. Too many boys fell in the South, and there weren't enough iron coffins. The Rebs rotted on the battlefield, but our young men had to be sent home."

I heard a quiver in Ziba's voice, but she caught herself. "The bodies of the Federal troops decayed in their wooden coffins, and the smell made transport impossible. The war forced doctors to embalm the dead in the surgeons' tents. Papa honed his skills on the battlefield. He headed the team of embalming surgeons who prepared President Lincoln's body after his murder. My dear father dreamed of a time when the common man would entrust the remains of his loved ones to those skilled in the funerary arts. People are seeking our services. After all, we can't have poor Uncle George stinking up the parlor, can we?"

Despite the presence of three clients in different states of the preservation process, laughter filled the room. Everybody except for me seemed quite gay. One would think we were having tea rather than pumping up a corpse with poison. Ziba snickered when she slipped a black leather apron over my head. "I don't want you to get embalming fluid on your new gown, dear."

The deceased lay on marble slabs bordered by

troughs on either side. A recently embalmed child lay on one slab. Her head rested on a wooden block. Her auburn locks awaited the final caress of a curling iron.

I turned from the dead tyke only to face the corpse of a young woman. The unfortunate still wore her bloodstained nightgown. Ziba pursed her lips into a grim line.

"The dear lady died in childbirth this morning."

Ziba took my hand and led me away from the poor creature. "Don't worry, she'll soon be cleansed of all the muck. We must thank the Lord her baby survived, and we won't have to place a tiny corpse in her arms."

Her words did not comfort me.

Mr. Greer pulled back a sheet covering a corpulent man who lay on the third slab, his chest and stomach exposed. The thick mustache and coarse stubbles on his chin contrasted with his thinning, pompadoured hair. From his smell, I guessed Mr. Greer had scrubbed down the body with Dr. Bram's soap followed by a bath of grain alcohol.

Ziba took my hand and placed it on the man's chest. "Touch him, Delight, don't be afraid." She held my hand in place. His body was cold to the touch. When I pulled my hand, Ziba placed it back on him.

"There's no circulation, Delight, no beating heart. The blood has stopped heating his body. You'll get used to it."

Never.

She released my hand. "Now, the real work of embalming will begin."

Mr. Greer flexed the decedent's hands, fingers, wrist, elbows, and shoulders, turning the corpse's head from side to side, up and down before placing it on the wooden pillow. His action piqued my curiosity. "Mr. Greer, what are you doing?"

Abby spoke up. "Massage rids the body of blood clots, the embalmer's bane. It relieves rigor and helps us drain the blood from the body."

Ziba scrutinized the dead man's face. "Our client needs a shave, but before we proceed, I must demolish an old wives' tale that persists even in our modern era. In some parts of New England, you'll hear stories of an exhumed body sporting a full beard on his once cleanshaven corpse. Some swear on their mothers' graves that the hair and nails of the dead grow after death. Utter hogwash, yet no matter how often we attempt to educate the public, falsehoods persist, and ignorance still prevails. The body withers, the tissue recedes, so nails and hair appear longer."

With her assured manner and intelligent hazel eyes, Abby appeared to be Ziba's most gifted pupil. She soaped the man's face then shaved it with the skill of a master barber. His mustache remained in place, but his skin shone as smooth as a summer peach. The poor man's mouth lolled open, his lips and jaw slack. Ziba gazed at the corpse and spoke in the gravest tones.

"Our client was a man of the law and never shut his mouth."

Clara laughed heartily. "Oh Madame Thorpe, you possess a great wit. You should be on the stage."

I knew Ziba felt it necessary to add levity to the proceedings, but I found her clowning distasteful.

Abby opened the deceased's mouth even wider, pulled up his upper lip, and sewed the mouth closed. Mr. Greer complimented her handiwork. "It requires a strong hand to sew through gums, tissue, and cartilage."

If I had not been on the verge of vomiting, I too would have applauded Abby. When she finished, the client's mouth was as natural in death as I am sure it had in life.

Ziba examined Abby's work. "Excellent, excellent, Abby. Some morticians favor placing a smile on the face of the dead, however, I'm not one of them. I find something unnatural about a grinning corpse."

She turned the man's head slightly to the left. "It's time to make the jugular incision, Mr. Greer."

He stepped forward, a surgeon's scalpel gleaming in his hand, and slashed the vein. As the blood flowed into the troughs, Mr. Greer explained the gruesome process. "During the war, young men often bled out on the field of battle. However, when someone dies a natural death, we must drain the blood from the body before we pump in the embalming fluid. Cut the jugular, and the blood will flow. An embalmer only utilizes the abdomen when—"

Ziba completed his words. "When the embalmers are odious belly-punching ruffians like Mr. McCarthy and his confederate, Mr. Hyde. Those scoundrels dare to call us 'throat slashers.' The incision should be at the jugular vein unless the deceased is a child or the body is too far gone for normal embalming."

She sighed dramatically as if she was playing Lady Macbeth. "Once, I wanted to study medicine, but like many of our sex, found that path closed to me. Luckily, I had another course for my life. Papa and Mr. Greer began schooling me in the holy art when I was twelve. In tribute to my parents, I'll ensure you are skilled in proper preservation methods—unlike those villainous oafs, McCarthy and Hyde, with their vulgar Irish funerals."

She held up a glass bottle with the words *Dr. Bram's Embalming Fluid* embossed on the label. "There are several kinds of fluid, but my preference is a mixture that includes arsenic."

"Arsenic? But it's a poison, one could die."

Ziba pursed her lips once again. "You can't poison the dead, dear girl, and believe me, we're mindful of the risks and work carefully. Arsenic was in wide use during the war, and the results were splendid. Of course, we do use other compounds from time to time."

She nodded to Mr. Greer, a grin on her lovely face. "Now it is time to see the work of a true artist."

Ziba whispered in reverential tones. "We use a gravity jar to drip in embalming fluid, a slow process, but today I've asked Mr. Greer to demonstrate with the hand pump we use for home visits."

Mr. Greer injected the fluid into the corpse, and the skin plumped with each squeeze. Ziba smiled in approval.

"No blood flows through his veins, and he's as white as driven snow, but a careful application of my special rouge will soon give him the rosy glow of life. Patsy will now demonstrate an essential part of our process, Delight. Watch carefully."

Ziba handed Patsy a long, sharp-tipped instrument connected to a hose and bulb syringe. "Would you demonstrate cavity embalming with the trocar?"

Patsy stood over the man's stomach, plunged the trocar into his body, and moved the implement back and forth, suctioning his body fluids. I retched and placed my handkerchief to my face to avoid vomiting, but then the room began to spin. The last voice I heard as I fell to the floor belonged to Ziba.

"Poor girl. That's what comes from lacing one's corset too tight."

Chapter 8

Purge

I revived after a few minutes and stared into Abby's concerned face. I had fainted for the second time in my life and was mortified at the thought it might become a daily occurrence. Clara fanned my face while Abby spooned hot, sugary tea into my mouth. She spoke in gentle tones.

"Don't worry about fainting, Delight. We've all done it at one time or another."

Clara nodded in agreement. "Yes, we all have. Madame Thorpe says fainting from time to time is part of the job."

Ziba stroked my hand. "Delight, I know this all has been a shock, but you seem reinvigorated. We must return to the lesson."

I nodded in agreement. "Yes of course. I vow to see the embalming through even if I faint again."

Patsy continued her task. After suctioning the bloody mess into the aspiration pump, she attached the trocar to the gravity jar and flooded the intestines with embalming fluid. I had never seen such a repugnant show, but Ziba seemed pleased at the result.

"I'm sure those villains at McCarthy and Hyde have no idea what a trocar is much less the proper way to use one. That is why we see purge spewing from those they touch."

At the mention of the word *purge*, the girls gasped in unison. Mr. Greer pursed his mouth then shook his head with such vigor one would have thought Ziba had uttered an expletive.

Ziba's beautiful face wrinkled as if she had sniffed something odious. "Purge is post-mortem evacuation, vile, smelly, and repellant. Papa and I once made the mistake of making a social call on McCarthy and Hyde's establishment. We had the purest of motives."

Clara gave her a mournful nod. "Of course you did, Madame Thorpe."

Ziba rewarded Clara with her most saintly smile. "The two scoundrels presided over a particularly vulgar funeral attended by carousers of the lowest type. The mourners were a bunch of blubbering drunks. By the end of the wake, few could stand without assistance." She paused for dramatic effect.

"The deceased, a beefy fellow, had died from apoplexy. They laid him out in a shabby coffin, his face rouged like a hussy in a bawdy house. Their parlor reeked of beer and cheap rum. Suddenly, his poor widow let out a blood-curdling scream, fierce enough to sober up the assemblage. The woman pointed to the corpse's face. Blood trickled out of his nose. The poor woman screamed again, 'My God, my poor dead husband is bleeding!' then fell into a dead faint."

Ziba's charges took in every word as if listening to the Holy Writ. "It wasn't blood, my friends. It was purge, discharge from his stomach working its way out of his orifices because they'd embalmed the poor man in a slipshod manner. Purge, because Hyde and McCarthy are nincompoops who know nothing of the holy art."

The room went silent for a moment then exploded in applause once again. Mr. Greer stepped forward and handed Ziba a needle and thread. "Madame Thorpe, please demonstrate the proper way to sew up the deceased's chest."

Ziba gave a nod in my direction. "We sew up the body to prevent embalming fluid from seeping onto his burial clothes."

My nausea returned, and Abby noticed my barely contained revulsion. "Delight, seamstresses ply their trade on every corner in Boston and barely eke out a living. We're putting our sewing skills to profitable use."

Ziba nodded in agreement. "Neat sewing and good lock stitching come in handy when embalming. A woman's skills are useful. We call this suture 'the purse string.' Papa had a fine hand as did my mother, but even they admitted my stitching was far better than theirs, didn't they, Mr. Greer?"

His head bobbed in agreement, and she continued her lecture. "Of course, the stitching at McCarthy and Hyde is crude and sloppy. I have it from unimpeachable sources that their inferior methods have ruined shrouds and casket linings. Please observe how I clean the incision with cotton then fill it with talc and a bit of sawdust to absorb excess moisture, unlike our competitors."

I did not turn away when she sutured the neck and chest cavity. "Delight, so far only Mr. Greer and Patsy have mastered this stitch, but the other ladies get better at it day by day."

To be honest, my stitching was better than Ziba's, but I was not about to demonstrate my sewing skills on a corpse. The lesson came to an end, but not soon enough for me. Mr. Greer set the corpse in the traditional position of the dead, right hand over the left wrist.

Ziba's face glowed. "Ladies, we've reached the end of our journey. We'll wash him once more with our fine scented soap, pack his nether orifice with cotton, and Mr. Greer will stitch it so his intestines won't slip out. Finally, he'll wrap the male member in cotton."

She placed her arms around the twins' shoulders. "Clara, powder and rouge him, and you, my dear Patsy, groom his hair, that is, what is left of it. Dress him in his fine suit, and this handsome fellow will rest for eternity in a beautiful mahogany coffin."

The class erupted in applause. Ziba and Mr. Greer bowed with a thespian flourish, then, as though on cue, Bride appeared at the foot of the stairs with Teddy in tow.

It shocked me to see a child brought into the chamber of horrors, but he giggled when the three girls encircled him and covered him with kisses. Bride whispered something to Ziba. My young aunt broke out into a joyous grin.

"Ladies, there's been an interesting turn of events. I've just received word that Mrs. Ellis Wentworth, of Beacon Hill, has expired and her daughter needs our services."

The girls applauded again. Ziba took my hand, a dazzling smile on her face. "We're so fortunate, Delight. Mr. Greer will prepare my buggy, and the students will finish the other embalming. We must be off."

The faces of the young ladies betrayed their disappointment, and why not? Ziba chose me rather than one of her students to accompany her.

Abby seemed especially upset and averted her face. I inched over to her, took her hand, and whispered, "I would gladly trade places with you."

My words seemed to comfort her. "Thank you, Delight." She gave me a sisterly hug before stepping away, her shoulders slumped in resignation.

I followed Ziba to the top of the stairs, imploring her all the while. "Ziba, any one of those girls has more experience than I do, and of course, there's Mr. Greer. Why not ask him?"

Her smile evaporated immediately. She whispered, clearly mindful of Mr. Greer's proximity. "Are you mad, you silly girl? Those snobs of Beacon Hill would never allow a colored man to touch a white woman, not even a dead one."

Chapter 9

Mrs. Wentworth's Fete

We zipped down Beacon Street in a physician's coupe, a marvel of comfort and speed. The carriage maker had painted it the color of polished slate and striped with a fine line of glazed carmine. Ziba held the reins, urging on a pair of chestnut geldings, and ignoring the glares of coachmen we passed along the way. "Father loved this carriage. They built it to his specifications. He'd be elated at the thought of my driving it."

The coup clattered over red brick and Belgian pavers. We passed massive four-story brick-and-stone row houses of fashionable Beacon Street, great homes with undulating bow fronts that shifted from light to dark, the effect called *chiaroscuro*. The beauty surrounding me could not assuage my distress, though Ziba tried her best to comfort me.

"You mustn't be anxious, Delight, you're quite fashionable in your new gown. Besides, your celestial music will distract the guests from the horrid condition of your hands."

I ignored her words of succor. "Why couldn't one of the girls have accompanied you, or possibly Bride?"

From her angry flick of the horse crop, I knew I had annoyed her. "Today, I needed an assistant with beauty and charm, which, unfortunately, excludes my young ladies. Although we live in one of the birthplaces of liberty, Bride is of mixed blood, and those hypocrites would never accept her. This will be your introduction to polite society. I promise to bring Abby in the future."

"Ziba, I'll surely faint if I see another dead person, and I wouldn't be of any help with the embalming."

She drove the horses even faster. "Faint? Pooh! Don't speak like a superstitious goose. Fainting is a luxury our patrons can afford, not us. Rest easy, you won't have to help me embalm Mrs. Wentworth. There's a lovely harp in Wentworth House, and you'll comfort the bereaved with your angelic music. Later, on home visits, you'll greet the families of the deceased, and sell them the finest caskets."

Ziba was either deaf or indifferent, but I continued pressing my case. "I'll do anything you ask, scrub, cook, play the harp, but I don't want to work with the dead."

She glowered like a sulky child. "Must I explain it again? Dr. Reeves, Charles's father, is an important man in this city. He has introduced me to the best families in Boston, giving me entry into the great homes of the city. I won't squander a golden opportunity."

The coupe stopped in the center of a courtyard on Beacon Street. A servant boy scrambled to grab the reins of the rig. Along the street, armies of Irish maids swept the marble steps of the grand three-tiered mansions.

Despite the cold, Beacon Street matrons, bundled in heavy woolens and furs, promenaded with entourages of nursemaids and handsomely appointed children.

We alighted from the carriage, and the servants stopped their duties to watch us. "There they are, Delight, minions who are grateful to trek up and down five flights of stairs day and night at the ring of a bell.

Imagine those poor nurses, cooks, and chambermaids slaving long hours for those who look down their long noses at them. My father embalmed captains of industry. He assured me, they die like the rest of us, and their blood is no bluer than ours."

Ziba pulled two large valises from beneath the seat and handed the heavy bags to me. She strode to the entry of a mammoth bow-front mansion the Wentworth family called home.

"There it is, Wentworth House, the Jewel of Boston. Mr. Richardson, the famed architect, converted two brownstones into a single mansion. Can you believe that aside from the servants, only two people lived here? Now, there's just one."

My arms strained from the weight of the bags, and the sheer size of the massive structure awed me. Ziba grabbed the elaborate bell pulley, and within seconds, a girl in a black uniform opened the door, her eyes and nose red from crying. Ziba handed her calling card to the tearful servant.

"Please tell Miss Wentworth that Madame Thorpe has arrived."

The servant led us through a foyer of Italian marble lined with potted ferns into a massive parlor. Ziba strode into the chamber as though she owned the place, but I stopped at the threshold stunned by its grandeur. All of Massachusetts knelt to Mrs. Ellis Wentworth who was renowned for her patronage of the arts and her vast collection of paintings and sculptures. Still, nothing prepared me for such magnificence.

Ziba spoke in hushed tones as she gestured to the opulence that surrounded us. "Mrs. Wentworth spent a fortune on those carved ceilings from an Italian villa. I'm told those furnishings once graced Napoleon Bonaparte's chambers in Paris."

She entered a sumptuous room, but I remained in the corridor. Persian rugs, in brilliant hues, covered the parquet floors. The divans and ordinary chairs were carved from teak and mahogany and upholstered in the finest satin damask. In the center of the room, surrounded by splendor, lay the corpse of a delicate woman of middle years. The body reclined on a swooning chaise, still clad in her night chemise and robe. Uniformed serving women stood at attention, their faces expressionless.

Charles, resplendent in a black frockcoat, stood above the chaise, arm in arm with a young woman who appeared to be no older than eighteen. She was as fragile as a porcelain doll, and her black velvet *toilette* set off her pale skin and hair to perfection.

Charles seemed the very picture of a solicitous friend. "Dear Miss Wentworth, please know Father did his best for your mother. Rest assured that she is now in the loving arms of Our Lord."

The blue veins in Miss Wentworth's waxen skin were visible despite a light dusting of rice powder. When she placed a handkerchief to her nose, it seemed as if the simple act of breathing exhausted her. Charles and Miss Wentworth exchanged a long, intense gaze then she placed a tiny hand on his. Anyone observing their private moment would note what an exquisite couple they made, so well-matched, so regal, so elegant.

I glanced at Ziba. From her pursed lips and brightly colored cheeks, it seemed that Charles's attention to the girl angered her. Charles had opened his heart to give succor to the poor creature in her time of need, yet Ziba greeted his generosity with jealousy. I bit my tongue to avoid reproaching her.

A young lady, tall, dark, and dressed in a tailored suit, hovered behind Miss Wentworth. She watched in silence.

Ziba's demeanor suddenly changed. She walked toward the fair beauty, her arms outstretched, concern etched on her face.

"Dear Miss Wentworth, may I express my condolences. I—dear Lord!"

Ziba caught sight of two men standing behind a huge potted palm, whispering together like conspirators. They sported oversized mustachios and muttonchops. Both were garbed in the vulgar plaid sack suits of men in commerce. She stormed over to them, her face flushed. "What are you scoundrels doing here?"

The taller of the two, a heavyset fellow with ginger hair, smirked. "This isn't your affair, Madame Thorpe."

The other, his balding pate covered with wisps of blonde hair, stepped forward. "We came to pay our respects."

I assumed they were the odious Mr. McCarthy and Hyde, the two blackhearts Ziba had railed against with such vehemence. Charles, seeing my aunt's anger, gave the men a curt nod and then whispered to Ziba. "Please remember where we are and behave accordingly."

His words quieted her, but another voice, masculine and resolute, commanded attention. "These villains showed up the moment they heard the poor woman was on her deathbed, like carrion smelling a fresh kill."

The speaker, a tall, distinguished gentleman, entered the room. Fair-haired with a trim mustache, he bore a marked resemblance to both Charles and Edgar. He must have been well into middle age, at least forty. I realized he was their father, the famed Dr. Reeves I'd heard so much about. Dr. Reeves gave the two embalmers a nasty scowl and positioned himself next to our fragile hostess.

"If Miss Wentworth hadn't intervened, I would have gladly thrashed them both within an inch of their lives." He took Miss Wentworth's tiny hand in his. "Dear Drusilla, they are vampires who will leave your mother as gray as a ghost, steal the gold from her teeth, and the rings from her fingers."

The distasteful words came from Dr. Reeves, but the heavyset man ignored him and glared at Ziba instead. "Those charges were never proved."

Miss Wentworth stepped away from the two interlopers as if their proximity would contaminate her. "Gentlemen, thank you for your concern, however, Madame Thorpe and I have already been corresponding for more than a fortnight. She'll prepare my mother for burial tomorrow."

Ziba turned from Miss Wentworth to Dr. Reeves, obviously shocked. "She's to be buried tomorrow? I assumed the body of so prominent a woman would lie in state for at least three days. May I inquire why such haste?"

Before the young woman could reply, Dr. Reeves spoke. "It isn't haste, my dear Mrs. Thorpe. Poor Miss Wentworth is wracked with grief and can't bear to be reminded of her great loss." He stroked our hostess's pale hand. "My darling girl, I'll have these rapscallions escorted from the premises."

Dr. Reeves summoned her butler with a flick of his other hand. "Show Mr. Hyde and Mr. McCarthy to the door."

McCarthy and Hyde turned to the grieving daughter and bowed low. As they exited, the taller embalmer hissed at Ziba, "Throat slasher."

Ziba replied to his rancorous comment with one of her own. "Gut picker."

Miss Wentworth, unaware of the exchange, sighed. "Dr. Reeves, Mrs. Thorpe, and Charles, I must take my leave. The day has been so taxing."

Before she departed, Ziba took the young woman's hand. "Thank you for your confidence, Miss Wentworth. I promise to do my best for your dear mother." The grieving girl nodded and walked off with the dark-haired young lady. Ziba watched them depart, a nasty smirk on her face.

I did not wish to draw attention to myself. Thankfully, no one had acknowledged my presence. Then, Dr. Reeves caught sight of me standing at the threshold. "My dear Ziba, is that lovely creature Ephraim's niece? I've heard so much about her. Please, ask her to enter."

Ziba called out. "Delight, wherever are your manners? Come in and meet Dr. Reeves."

I took a hesitant step into the room, still weighed down by the supplies. Charles raced over, grabbed the bags from me, and placed them next to the chaise. He led me to Dr. Reeves. "Father, this is the young lady I told you about."

Dr. Reeves bowed before kissing my hand. "What an enchanting girl. How I wish we could have met under better circumstances."

I attempted a smile. "Thank you, sir." Try as I might, I could not help myself from staring at Mrs. Wentworth's corpse. Her eyes and mouth remained open, her face contorted in pain. I wanted to flee, yet stayed rooted in place, and felt the color draining from my face.

Ziba flexed the corpse's arm and then declared triumphantly, "Still warm."

Dr. Reeves bent over the chaise, gazed into Mrs. Wentworth's distorted visage, and stroked her brow.

"This angelic woman took her final breath just before you arrived. She sat at death's door when I sent for you. Mercifully, the Lord took her before she suffered more pain."

Ziba clasped her hands together. "Merciful indeed. The closer to death, the better the results will be. It's time to begin our work. I'll need basins, clean towels, and hot water."

A servant rushed from the room. Charles glanced in my direction, his green eyes twinkling, but he appeared vexed when he turned to my young aunt. "Ziba, didn't we agree to wait before you exposed Delight to embalming?"

Ziba turned to him, a pout on her lovely face. "You can be so tedious, Charles. Delight observed an embalming this morning and survived." She pointed to a beautiful hand-carved harp sitting amidst a mass of palms. "Besides, Miss Wentworth has that lovely instrument for her to play."

Dr. Reeves smiled at Ziba before taking my hand in his. "Perhaps it would be better if the charming Miss Thorpe leaves the room before the embalming begins."

Ziba answered with a shake of her head. "How is she going to learn without observing?"

She opened one of her cases and laid out the embalming tools on a nearby tea table. Two young maids entered carrying porcelain basins, one filled with steaming water, the other empty.

Ziba signaled to the serving girl holding the full basin, and the girl inched toward the chaise. She slashed open Mrs. Wentworth's nightgown. The poor servant and I both gasped at the mass of puckered flesh on Mrs. Wentworth's left breast, a discolored clump of purplish skin, the open wound oozing puss.

Despite the fragrance of burning incense and lavender, the sticky odor of disease caused bile to rise to my throat. The serving girls stood wide-eyed at the sight. How I pitied the poor creatures since they were dutybound to stay in place. I pressed my handkerchief to my lips, praying I would not vomit. "Please excuse me, but I think I'll be sick."

Dr. Reeves took my arm and led me toward the door. "She didn't have an easy death. It would be best if you left, Miss Thorpe."

Ziba glanced at me. "You're a bit green around the gills, poppet. A servant will attend to you."

As I stumbled out of the room, I heard Dr. Reeves's voice. "My dear Mrs. Thorpe, I prefer something other than arsenic for the embalming and brought my own solution."

"Very well, Dr. Reeves."

How strange. That very morning, Ziba had extolled the virtues of arsenic. I wondered why she did not argue for it but, I could not ask. My heaving stomach made me fear I might ruin the beautiful carpets along with Ziba's chance of success.

I rushed down the hushed corridor. A whimper from a darkened alcove followed by whispers and sighs slowed my pace. A soft female voice said, "Hush, my darling. Please don't cry."

I peeked into the niche and saw two figures locked in an embrace. The dark-haired woman nuzzled Miss Wentworth's neck. She turned the grief-stricken girl's face to her own and then kissed her on the mouth. The ardor of their embrace confused me, for I had not seen such fire or such passion between two girls before. The girls from my quilting circle shared a deep affection but never displayed it in such an enthusiastic manner.

I tiptoed past so as not to disturb them but stopped when a hand touched my shoulder. "Delight."

I turned to face Charles, and my heart fluttered.

He smiled at the two women and then spoke in a murmur. "Poor Miss Wentworth required comforting in her hour of grief. Thankfully, her friend offered solace."

Charles took my arm and led me farther down the corridor to another ostentatious drawing room. A diminutive child maid of no more than twelve stood at silent attention. He led me to a chaise and took a step back. "You're splendid in your lovely frock."

I realized the futility of trying to conceal my blushes. "You could turn a girl's head with such pretty words, Charles."

"Is it possible to turn her head in my direction?"

I averted my face, afraid I might giggle at his flattery. Words escaped me, and when he took a seat next to me on the settee and placed his hand over mine, I thought I would swoon.

He stared into my eyes, all playfulness abandoned. "Dear girl, please promise me you'll forgive your aunt for bringing you. I advised against it, but she continued to ignore me. She's a very headstrong young woman. She and Father can finish with Mrs. Wentworth before the viewing. Try to survive until then. You'll meet

Boston's patrician families. I'm afraid they aren't a friendly lot, but I'll be nearby. Please excuse me, my dear."

Charles stood, bowed, and then took his leave. The little servant and I were alone in the massive room. We exchanged a shy glance then she walked away.

Chapter 10

Boston Bluebloods

That afternoon, the *crème de la crème* of Boston society filled Mrs. Wentworth's drawing room. The Cabots, Otis Grays, Lowells, Lodges, and Bowdoins, the city's nobility, encircled the chaise, inspecting the remains of the late *doyenne*. Boston's august mayor, his lips quivering beneath an impressive white walrus mustache, perused the body and declared, "With the death of Mrs. Wentworth, our city has lost its greatest benefactor."

The gentlemen wore sober morning suits, the uniform of the day. The ladies attired themselves in somber black gowns with elaborate furbelows, and elegant bonnets covering their patrician heads. Most of the thin-lipped matrons had the waxen complexions of cadavers.

Ziba nodded to a group of women enjoying tea. "The ladies achieve their ghastly pallor by rigorous use of White Delight Face Wash and Orange Flower Skin Crème." She pointed to a delicate woman with skin whiter than an albino. "You see that lady? I have it on the best authority that she uses a concoction of rice powder blended with arsenic, lead, and pulverized eggshells on her skin. Mark my words, she'll be our client soon enough."

Mrs. Ellis Wentworth lay in state in an ivory lace *toilette*, unseasonable but flattering, her chestnut hair elegantly coiffed. Ziba had skillfully exorcised all signs of the poor woman's agony. Although my young aunt had railed against it, she fixed Mrs. Wentworth's mouth into a placid smile. Our late hostess had transformed her home into the finest museum in Boston. In death, she had become another *object d' art*.

Unfortunately, the servants had positioned the harp in full view of the corpse, but I remained in Charles's line of vision. He kept his eyes on me even as he chatted with several young ladies from the finest families who circled him, giggling as they used their feminine wiles. A handsome young lady pushed the girls aside and seated herself on the settee next to him. She tilted her blonde head, simpered sweetly, and batted her eyelashes. The pair were in such proximity to me that I could not stop myself from eavesdropping. "Charlie, I detest these affairs."

"Why, sweet girl?"

The young lady pouted her answer. "Because they bore me so. There's no gaiety, no dancing. I don't like wearing black or dead people. I barely knew Mrs. Ellis Wentworth, but Mama said I must accompany her because the best people would be here. Pooh, if I wished to be near the dead, I would have gone with my friends to see the medium, Margaret Fox. It sounds so exciting. Everyone in Boston has seen her except me because my mother won't permit it. Mama can be so tedious."

Charles seemed amused and stifled a smile. "Shall we speak of brighter things? Your brother told me you just returned from the Continent. It must have been a great adventure."

The girl simpered and fluttered her eyes. Her manner may have enchanted armies of other Harvard boys but did not appear to have the same effect on Charles. "I hated it, Charlie. I told Papa that I never shall go back. Everything in Europe is old and dirty with all those smelly foreigners speaking their silly languages. I was bored the entire time."

Charles placed a gentle hand on hers, a hint of a smile dancing across his lips. "My poor lamb." He turned in my direction and caught my eye. Perhaps a gas jet flickered, but I could have sworn he winked at me. I averted my head and continued playing.

Dr. Reeves strolled over, scrutinized the room, then turned to me, his eyes sparkling. "Miss Thorpe, I'm a longtime friend of the Bram family. I served with Dr. Bram and your uncle Ephraim in the War of the Rebellion and met your late father on more than one occasion. I recently learned of your great loss."

He glanced at Ziba who engaged Miss Wentworth in conversation and at that moment, appeared the very soul of empathy.

"It's been a difficult time for you both. You, a mere slip of a girl, and poor Ziba, a child I've known since she was a tot. The responsibilities she's taken on her delicate shoulders after your uncle's untimely death would kill the average man."

A quartet of somber young fellows entered the room. The doctor stopped speaking the moment he saw the youths. The four acknowledged Charles with polite nods, made their way to the chaise, and bowed their heads over Mrs. Wentworth's corpse. They whispered among themselves.

Dr. Reeves's attention pivoted to the young men.

"Those chaps are Harvard boys, Charlie's law school chums, sterling fellows unaccustomed to such grandeur. I should speak to them before they make buffoons of themselves."

He turned back to me, a broad smile on his lips. "My dear, please excuse me. I'll be dining at your aunt's table in two nights, Miss Thorpe. We'll continue our conversation then."

Ziba had not mentioned having a guest for dinner. "I'll look forward to it, Dr. Reeves."

The good doctor gave me a final nod before joining the students. He greeted them warmly with handshakes then clustered with the boys, prodding them to mingle with the other mourners. Charles continued chatting with the girl.

****

Ziba drove the coupe down Commonwealth Avenue, giggling like a schoolgirl the entire time. Unfortunately, she could not infect me with her high spirits.

"Did you hear the comments about how life-like Mrs. Wentworth was? One of the matrons swore Mrs. Wentworth never looked so beautiful, even more radiant in death than when she was breathing. Many commented on the wondrous music too. I noted that every eye in the room was on you, dear Delight. More than one gentleman remarked about the heavenly creature playing the harp."

I said nothing. From their snide glances, most of the women appeared to have dismissed me as trade, one step above a servant. The men who looked my way appraised me with less than gentlemanly eyes. The shy gentility of the Harvard fellows remained the afternoon's only pleasant moment aside from seeing Charles. Ziba might be comfortable with the Boston gentry, but I doubted I would ever be.

Ziba's eyes sparkled, and her face glowed, not from rouge or powder, but from pride in the compliments on her artistry.

"It was my greatest triumph, though I must admit I'm rather peeved that Miss Wentworth wouldn't allow us to embalm her mother at Bram House. We could have performed miracles, but what does it matter anyway? They'll enshroud her tomorrow and bury her like last week's roast beef. I took such pains with the preservation too. The viewing could have lasted three days."

I remained silent as she chattered away. In God's truth, her triumph so consumed her I could have fallen into a fit and frothed at the mouth without her noticing.

"We owe our success to Dr. Reeves. He introduced us to his social circle. He'll be joining us for dinner in two days, along with Charles and Edgar, so you must wear another of the new gowns."

"Charles will be joining us?" My mood lifted in an instant.

"Yes, he will. Can you believe he had an understanding with Miss Wentworth?"

Charles and Miss Wentworth? I remembered her anger at Charles's kindness to the young lady. Could Ziba view him as a suitor after her period of mourning ended? He seemed very much a part of Boston society. She did not appear the least concerned.

Ziba pushed the horses even faster. "Oh yes, my dear, it's true. The late Mrs. Wentworth wanted him for a son-in-law, and for a brief time, he and Miss Wentworth were quite the couple, inseparable. Everyone in Boston thought they'd marry one day. Of course, they were too young. To be honest, if it weren't for their families pushing the union, I doubt Charles would ever have paid any attention to that bloodless scarecrow."

She chuckled and smirked like a child with a great secret. "Believe me, dear girl, things have changed in that regard."

I remained silent. How could I have ever entertained the fantasy that a man of Charles's station would ever be interested in me? The thought of his eminent marriage to Miss Wentworth was too overwhelming to consider. I felt like a fool.

Ziba flicked the horsewhip and then pointed to a brick edifice built in the Georgian style. "Delight, there's Faneuil Hall."

Every child in Massachusetts knew Faneuil Hall. My spirits lifted the moment I peered out the carriage window and saw the famed grasshopper weathervane atop the temple of free speech. We moved close enough for me to read the colorful gonfalon splashed across the entrance, *The American Woman Suffrage Association Presents Famed Speaker, Lucy Stone.*

I shrieked in joy. "Lucy Stone is speaking. How wonderful!"

Ziba pushed the horses further. "If I'd known her name would bring a smile to your face, I'd have brought you here earlier."

Throngs massed into the hall, and the frigid air crackled with electricity, anger, and expectation. The sounds from the street almost drowned out a group of ladies from the Temperance Society marching in lockstep. A young woman pounded the bass drum with such abandon I feared she would have a fit of apoplexy.

A group of suffragists, male and female, stood in front of the building exhorting everyone to join them in the celebration of the power of womanhood. Unfortunately, a gang of bullyboys hurled epithets at everyone who entered the hall.

"Go home, you damned trollops!"

The crowd ignored their fruitless efforts, but the faces of the young men flared red with rage. "Ziba, we should leave before there's a fight."

She cackled at the surging crowd. "Leave? Why would I leave? Isn't it exciting? If fisticuffs break out, I'll write about it in my journal. I keep all my adventures there."

Ziba's tittering stopped when a young man rushed our carriage, causing the horses to bolt. "Suffragist whores!"

She struck the fellow across the face with the horsewhip and spurred the steeds on, almost running the rapscallion down as we headed away from the hall.

"Thrilling wasn't it?"

I could barely catch my breath. My head throbbed so violently that I could not answer. Ziba mistook my silence for sullenness.

"Oh pooh, Delight, do I see another grumpy face? Well, I'll tell a joke, that is what I'll do. Even you will enjoy this one. Beethoven died, and they buried him. A week later, the town rum pot was walking through the cemetery, and heard a strange noise coming from Mr. Beethoven's grave. Terrified, the souse ran off and fetched a priest. The priest bent close to the grave and heard music. It frightened the cleric, so he ran and roused the town magistrate. When the magistrate arrived, he listened for a moment and said, 'Ah, yes, that's

Beethoven's Ninth Symphony, being played backward.' He listened a while longer and said, 'That's the Eighth Symphony, and it's backward, too. It's most puzzling.' He kept listening. 'And now the Seventh, the Sixth, the Fifth—' Suddenly, he stood up and announced to the crowd gathering in the cemetery. 'My fellow citizens, there's nothing to worry about. It's just Beethoven— decomposing!'"

Ziba chortled all the way to Bram House.

Chapter 11

The Dinner Party

I spent an uneventful second night in Boston with neither dreams nor unwelcome visitors. The unsettling reality of bodies in the parlor no longer disturbed me, yet, from the moment I awoke, I could not chase memories of my village from my thoughts. It had been a place of laughter, white birch trees, the perfume of the sea and balsam, brilliant summer skies. Unfortunately, other recollections intruded. I remembered the vile stench of the sick room, the moaning of those about to die, then the sound I most feared, the death rattle.

In the late morning, I watched a grand funeral procession of elegant carriages and fine horses snake its way through the cemetery. Mrs. Ellis Wentworth would be resting in her family plot by the afternoon. Charles would stand graveside, surrounded by a coterie of the belles of Boston, with the delicate Miss Wentworth on his arm. The thought of him in the company of such an elegant girl was too much to bear.

I mentioned the burial at supper and his attention to Miss Wentworth, but Ziba remained adamant in her denial of a romantic attachment between the two. "Drusilla Wentworth is nothing to Charles."

I managed to smile while Ziba chattered away about her upcoming dinner party. "Delight, my goosy, you must wear the lovely wine-colored *toilette* in your wardrobe."

She referred to a gown pilfered from poor Miss Elda Rice. It made no difference that the gown belonged to a dead girl. It was beautiful, and for once in my life, I had no guilt about enjoying it.

"But the color is wrong for mourning."

Although I did not expect Ziba to wear black for two years, the celebration seemed premature.

She cooed sweetly, barely able to contain her elation. "Delight, I know the hue is inappropriate, but humor me just this once. Only our male guests and the serving girls will wear black tomorrow night. I've invited my embalming ladies to join us too. It's to be a celebration of your arrival in Boston and our new life, my darling. For one evening, we'll forget mourning and sadness. We have the rest of our lives for tears. Oh, my dear girl, I'm so excited about dinner tomorrow. It will be a night to remember."

****

The next day, with Bram House closed to clients, Bride's relations swept and scrubbed every room and polished the crystal and silver to a high sheen. They covered the monstrous table with freshly laundered Belgian linen, gleaming China, and the best serving pieces. On Ziba's orders, she had spared no expense for food and wine. I imagined she had bullied and haggled with every butcher and greengrocer in town.

Ziba rushed about the house aflutter with excitement, inspecting every plate, napkin, table runner, and piece of stemware. Finally, after scrutinizing the preparations, she retired to her bedchamber to complete her elaborate dress and *maquillage*. Bride banished

Teddy to the stables under Mr. Greer's vigilant eyes.

I thanked the Lord that Ziba had not subjected the kitchen to her love of ornamentation. Laundry bluing tinted the walls pale indigo, the lower half covered with a dado of wainscoting. Bride packed the whitewashed cupboards with all manner of modern convenience—a coffee roaster, egg basket, spice mill, a cast iron spider skillet, fish kettle, and vegetable steamer. A fine icebox stood at one end of the room, a large and splendid cast iron stove at the other, while another stove sat in the nearby scullery.

Hecuba patrolled the massive room, on the hunt for rats and mice, and Bride repaid her with generous portions of cod and reluctant admiration. "She's a monstrous evil beast, but no one can deny she's the best mouser in Boston."

The homey kitchen warmed me to my soul. When I volunteered to assist in the preparations for the evening's festivities, I found myself barred by a stone-faced Bride. "We don't need no help, miss."

How could they turn down a willing hand? "But why not, Bride? No one has ever complained about my cooking. I can pluck a chicken in the wink of an eye, and you'll never taste a better apple cobbler than mine."

She rolled up her sleeves revealing burn marks on her forearms and hands, a silent testament to her years of slaving in Boston's great kitchens. "I've been in service since the age of eleven and have a scar for every year. The mistress will have my head if you burn yourself."

At least she did not begrudge me hot water and towels for my bath. I soaked in the scullery's cast iron tub and listened as Bride and the serving girls chattered among themselves. The girl with the harelip mentioned working as a day laborer at Wentworth House. "What a grand mansion it is."

Bride harrumphed before rolling her eyes up to the ceiling. "If you'd seen how dirty that kitchen is, you'd never eat there. All the great houses on Beacon Hill have kitchens filthy with grease and soot. At night, the floors come alive with vermin, and mice crawl up the pipes and get into the water closets. I heard one cook on Beacon Street kept hedgehogs and let them out at night to eat those nasty little beasties. There's none here."

Beacon Hill, hedgehogs, and mice did not concern me. Perhaps the festivities would take my mind off my constant companion, morbidity.

I left the bath and dried myself in the warmth of the scullery stove. A tiny hand, the size of a child's, touched my shoulder. I turned to the mute serving girl, an unreadable expression on her delicate face. She held out a comb. I settled in a wicker chair, took a deep breath, and let her dress my hair for the evening ahead.

****

The embalming girls arrived first, courtesy of Mr. Greer who transported them in the Bram hearse. The foyer crackled with excitement. The young ladies scented themselves with lilac water, and then rouged, powdered, and pomaded. They had dressed in fine gowns purchased from the families of dead clients.

Abby's emerald velvet bodice enhanced the beauty of her chestnut hair. For once, the twins had not dressed identically. Clara garbed herself in a sleeveless periwinkle blue satin gown that accented her eyes and red hair. Patsy wore peach satin, her elaborate brocade skirt shot through with golden straw embroidery.

I wore Miss Elda Rice's gown of claret organza with

velvet panels in the bodice and skirt. My mother's best earrings of garnet and rose gold gleamed from my ears. A choker of copper and brass, my parents' dark hair intertwined into a rosette, encircled my neck.

Patsy rushed and took my hand. "Delight, you look beautiful."

Clara gave a nod of agreement. "This is the most exciting night of my life. To be gifted with these marvelous gowns and whisked away in a carriage, even if the carriage is a hearse, is a wondrous thing."

Abby stroked the velvet inserts of my bodice. "Such a splendid color." She picked up her skirts and twirled around the entryway like a green dervish. "Can you believe our good fortune? Madame Thorpe gave us these *toilettes*. Of course, the former owners are deceased, but my motto is waste not, want not."

The twins tittered in agreement.

Ziba's generosity had not extended to Mr. Greer, her chief embalmer, something I regretted, but did not dare to address. Still, I decided to enjoy the evening with my new friends. "My dear friends, you are all so lovely tonight."

The girls broke into giggles, and I had a pang of remembrance for my friends who had died.

Clara inspected the alcove and then spoke in a whisper. "This is so grand. I fear I'll throw up my dinner. I've never attended a formal dinner."

Abby fiddled with her gloves. "You won't throw up, Clara. We've all read Mrs. Hartley's *Book of Etiquette* so many times we've engraved it in our memories. We know what forks to use and how to behave. Just follow Madame Thorpe's example and be at your most charming."

At precisely seven o'clock on the dot, the bell chimed. I peeked into the alcove just as Dr. Reeves strode into Bram House followed by his sons. The three were sartorial elegance personified, but Charles outshone the other two, an Adonis in a black tailcoat. Edgar had also primped for the evening and wore a formal suit, his hair carefully pomaded with Macassar oil. He carried a violin case, in the hope of serenading us at dinner.

I whispered to the girls. "Now that the men are here, I must leave you. Ziba swears Dr. Reeves and Charles considered punctuality a cardinal virtue. Good luck, my friends."

I watched as the girls made a slow promenade to the alcove where the Reeves family stood in wait. Dr. Reeves, ever the gentleman, kissed each gloved hand. At five minutes past seven o'clock, Ziba floated down the staircase in a cloud of French perfume. She wore a pale blue gown, the décolletage low enough to reveal her bosom. Charles gasped when he saw her.

Some might consider her gown unsuitable for a twenty-year-old widow, but I have no doubt after her marriage to my uncle, she relished her innocent conquests. The men inhaled in unison, and Charles couldn't take his eyes off her. The embalming girls applauded her entrance, and Dr. Reeves spoke for all.

"Aphrodite has just descended from Mount Olympus."

I dashed into the dining room to take my place behind my harp. Bride had surrounded my instrument with a semi-circle of lit candles, and I moved with care to avoid igniting my skirt. My *glissando* signaled the guests to enter, the good doctor at Ziba's arm. She had ordered an evening of enchantment and enchanting it would be.

Edgar joined me on his violin as I played a nocturne by Mr. Chopin. Our communication through music had none of the discomforts of our spoken conversation. Abby, the twins, Dr. Reeves, and Charles gave us their rapt attention, but Ziba prattled away throughout.

"Delight has been hiding in the kitchen all day. One would think she was a scullery maid. I'm afraid we can take the girl out of the country but can't take the country out of the girl."

Dr. Reeves snickered at Ziba's remark, Abby and the twins whispered among themselves, but Charles's attention remained fixed on Edgar and me. When our duet ended, our small audience applauded with great enthusiasm. Charles jumped to his feet. "Bravo. Bravo!" And the girls joined him.

Edgar and I took our seats at the grotesque slab of a dining table.

Two of Bride's minions, the mute, and the girl with the crossed eyes, stood at rapt attention. They wore crisp black uniforms and white gloves, the smells of the kitchen scrubbed away with embalmer's soap. Ziba played the minx, batting her lashes, flirting with the gentlemen, clearly relishing her role as grand hostess.

"Thank you all for sharing our humble fare."

Dr. Reeves snickered as he unfolded his napkin.

"Humble fare indeed, you've set a table fit for the Czar. Only last week I endured dining *a la Russe*, a complex affair that went on interminably. Such feasts test one's endurance. I can't begin to tell you how I've anticipated this meal."

Charles's eyes sparkled as he regaled us with a

story. "Add the sin of snobbery to gluttony, ladies. One of Boston's finer gentlemen's clubs was serving a dinner of Herculean proportions when a fire broke out in the kitchen. Flames engulfed the place, yet when the fire brigade arrived, the majordomo insisted they use the servants' entrance."

The room erupted into laughter. The two serving girls barely contained their titters. Charles took a sip of his wine, winked at me, and went on with his story. "The old windbags continued dining during the blaze. Unfortunately, the place didn't burn to the ground, and they saved the kitchen. The club continues to serve the worst food in Boston to this day."

Ziba pouted seductively then placed her hand over Charles's. "What an amusing story. Dear Charles, you and your father dine so often on Beacon Hill that you forget even we rustics know about the better things in life. Our Mrs. Greer is the most talented cook in Massachusetts."

She turned to me with a smirk. "Delight, did I tell you that Dr. Reeves has attempted on more than one occasion to spirit Bride away, but I wouldn't hear of it."

More laughter, then Ziba lifted a gloved hand, and the maids began serving from gleaming platters sitting at the end of the great table. There would be seven courses complete with an *après* dessert savory, an ostentatious show.

Conversation clipped along most cordially until Dr. Reeves raised the subject of the war.

"I completed my medical degrees in '63, the youngest in my class. When the insurrection broke out, I enlisted right away. Those were heady days before the reality of the war intruded. We were innocent boys thrilled at the prospect of battling Johnny Reb. I remember when Bob Shaw's colored regiment proudly marched down Beacon Street. Everyone was overjoyed, that is until those copperheads at the Somerset Club hissed at those brave young men because of the color of their skin."

He pounded the table, and even in the dim candlelight, we saw his face had turned scarlet. "I swear if Dr. Bram hadn't restrained me, I would have horsewhipped every one of those Rebel-loving bastards!"

Dr. Reeves suddenly rose from his chair. "I should have killed them all!"

Silence enveloped the room.

Chapter 12

The Dinner

No one said a word for at least a minute while we tried to comprehend the reason for Dr. Reeves's outburst. The serving girls stared at the table, their faces as inscrutable as sculptures carved in granite. Clara and Patsy grasped each other's hands. Mrs. Harley's etiquette lessons had not prepared them for such a violent outburst. Abby and Ziba averted their faces while Edgar examined his plate.

Only Charles dared to speak. "But Dr. Bram did restrain you, Father, and no one died that day. Some Somerset members were angry enough to decamp and start the Union Club across the street. Boston is all the better for it."

Dr. Reeves took a large gulp of wine. "Yes, yes, of course, Charlie, you're right."

The good doctor took his seat once again, a sheepish expression on his face. "Please excuse my outburst, ladies."

The gay mood returned, and everyone, apart from Edgar, appeared to savor the meal. Edgar picked at his food and stared at me with burning eyes. Attention from such a handsome young fellow was flattering, but I found his interest disconcerting and could not return his gaze.

I ignored Edgar and imitated Dr. Reeves and Charles

as they accepted or declined dishes. Dinner went swimmingly until Ziba steered the conversation toward work.

"I must compliment Dr. Reeves. He was invaluable when I embalmed poor Mrs. Wentworth. Her illness had left the poor woman so emaciated I couldn't find the vein. Mr. Greer might have found it, but I couldn't. Thank the Lord, Dr. Reeves lifted it in the wink of an eye without spilling a drop of blood. It reminded me of my dear Papa. Dressed in his best frock coat, he could embalm three stout men then go out to supper with no one the wiser."

Once again, the room fell silent. Charles appeared none too pleased with Ziba's comments and turned to me with a smile. "Miss Thorpe, I've been informed you have another talent besides your musical gift. Perhaps you will share it with us."

He began speaking French in the most elegant accent I'd ever heard. "*Votre tante m'a revelé ton secret: elle m'a dit que vous parlez Français.* Your aunt revealed your secret. You speak French."

I answered in my tentative French. "*Oui, je parle Français.* Yes, I speak French." The mood turned jolly once again.

Clara applauded with great enthusiasm. "I love to hear French spoken, though I must confess, I don't understand a word of it. Still, it is such a splendid language."

Abby and Patsy nodded in agreement. Charles toasted me with his wineglass.

Edgar, emboldened by our exchange, said, "I detect a Quebec accent, Miss Thorpe."

The wine I had sampled loosened my tongue and I

could not resist addressing Edgar in a light-hearted manner. I made a jest—in French.

"*Chèr Edgar, je prie que mon accent Quebecois t'a pas offensé les oreilles Européennes*—Dear Edgar, I pray my Quebecois accent hasn't offended your European ears."

Everyone chuckled, everyone, that is, except Ziba. Her lips curled in another pout, and we ignored her. Something I said amused them, me, Old Sobersides. Have I developed a sense of humor? In the future, would people remark on my wit? A grand thought indeed.

Dr. Reeves replied in English. "My darling girl, your accent can be remedied by one visit to Paris, something I'd be most happy to arrange."

His sons applauded, the girls tittered, and everyone appeared quite jolly. Suddenly, Ziba struck her wine goblet with a dessert spoon. She hit it with so much fury I feared the glass would shatter, but it did not. She spoke through clenched teeth. "Dr. Reeves, Charles, Edgar, and young ladies, not everyone at this table speaks French. Some of us learned the classical languages, Latin and Greek. *Tempus fugit*. It's time for dessert."

Charles spoke up, a sheepish expression on his face. "Oh dear me, Ziba. Delight speaks French so well that it allows us all to practice. Will you ever forgive us?"

He grinned, Ziba laughed, and the girls' goblets clinked in a toast. Edgar simpered, Dr. Reeves guffawed, all rancor forgotten. Dr. Reeves lifted his wineglass and saluted her. "Compliments are in order for the delicious fare, my dear girl."

Ziba's gaiety returned. "Thank you. We worked our fingers to the bone to ensure all would enjoy it."

She pouted once again when she turned to me.

"Delight, you naughty girl, you barely touched dinner. I swear you don't eat enough to feed a gnat."

My seams nearly burst from all the food I had consumed. Why did Ziba feel the need to chastise me?

She took an angry sip of wine and continued her assault. "Now we have you here at Bram House, we'll fatten you up. Otherwise, you shall soon resemble poor Mrs. Ellis Wentworth." Ziba placed her hand over Charles's. "Let's have dessert, shall we?"

The last course consisted of Charlotte Russe, Boston crème pie, coffee, and Madeira wine accompanied by a savory called Angels on Horseback made from spiced oysters wrapped in bacon. I tasted a bit of the Charlotte Russe, all the while ignoring Edgar who continued to moon at me like a lovesick pup.

Dr. Reeves sat back in his chair, took a sip of Madeira, and then grunted with overstuffed satisfaction.

"Dinner was as perfect as any I have eaten in the city."

Abby gave a nod. "I can bear witness to Mrs. Greer's magnificent cooking since we dine here every day."

I imagined Bride would think her dinner far better than any served on Beacon Hill. No doubt, fresher, free of soot or the intrusion from the four-legged beasties that cooks sometimes fished out of dishes they later served to unsuspecting guests.

The serving girls swept up the plates and rushed off to the kitchen. They returned and placed crystal bowls filled with perfumed water on the table. Clara suddenly gave a loud, unladylike belch. Her face turned scarlet.

"Please excuse me."

She broke out in tears. "I'm mortified, simply

mortified."

Charles, a solemn expression on his face, returned her belch with a louder one of his own. "Don't be mortified, dear girl."

The massive room broke out in raucous laughter. Clara dried her tears, and relaxed silence enveloped the room. As much as I was enjoying the evening, I longed for the moment when I could finally unfasten my corset. Charles appeared ready for a nap. A satiated Dr. Reeves sat back in his chair, a broad smile on his face. "Ladies, would it offend you if I smoked? I feel so at home here."

Ziba nodded her approval, and the girls joined in unison. "Yes, of course, Dr. Reeves." Patsy summoned boldness I did not know she possessed. "I find smoking so very manly, dear Dr. Reeves."

He removed a pencil-thin cigarillo from his breast pocket and lit it. "A tobacconist in Havana hand rolls them from Cuba's most aromatic harvest then blends them with vanilla for scent and flavor. Unlike Patsy, my dear wife considered smoking a vile habit, but this fragrance pleases the ladies."

Dr. Reeves savored his smoke and puffed a series of smoke rings. The girls and I followed them up to the ceiling with our eyes, marveling at the large circles floating in the air.

Abby seemed transfixed. "How did you do that, Dr. Reeves?"

He puffed another. "A frivolous parlor trick I learned in my college fraternity. It's my secret, but perhaps, one day I'll show you how it is done."

Abby's eyes remained on a halo of smoke wafting up to the ceiling. "Dr. Reeves, do the grand ladies in Boston smoke cigarillos?"

He chuckled and shifted in his chair. "I've met a few who do."

We settled in place, sated, content to watch the perfumed smoke ascend to the ceiling. For one moment, I had put aside the sadness of the past month, the loss of those I loved, and even the corpses in the drawing room. Then, from my periphery, I noticed Edgar exchange a nervous glance with his father. He threw his napkin to the table. "Delight, have you heard the history of Bram House?"

Edgar paused then spoke in a rush. "There are stories about Bram House that you may not be aware of. Mr. Browning built his mansion above a graveyard built in Plymouth times. I've been told they buried a Puritan girl alive. She revived in her coffin and screamed, waking the groundskeeper. Upon opening the casket, he found that in her desperation, she'd torn away her shroud. It's said that when night falls, she walks the halls of Bram House, wailing her lament."

Edgar gave his father another glance once and threw back his Madeira. What a dreadful end to such a lovely evening. The girls looked from one to another, confused. I thought of my weeping visitor and my heart began to palpitate. Charles must have noted my distress, for he left his chair, knelt at my side, and took my hand.

Ziba's face went ashen. She glanced at Dr. Reeves from the corner of her eye. "What has possessed you to tell that horrible story, Edgar?"

She turned to me with a look of concern. "Dear, don't listen to him. Ask the girls, ask Bride, ask Mr. Greer. It isn't true. I swear it isn't true."

Abby mustered her courage. "Delight, it's balderdash."

Dr. Reeves threw his napkin onto the table and glared at Edgar. "This is an unfortunate end to a delightful dinner. I'm afraid my poor son can't handle spirits, though he still persists in drinking."

Dr. Reeves's explanation did not stop Ziba from railing at his son. "Have you gone mad, Edgar Reeves, filling Delight's head with such twaddle?"

The good doctor walked over to my chair and placed a reassuring hand on my shoulder. "My poor child, yes, the wine has gone to Eddie's head, but truthfully, Bram House is no place for you and never will be."

Ziba glared at the good doctor. "Bram House is her home."

He ignored her. "We'll find you other lodgings, Delight. Perhaps a lovely finishing school—"

Ziba rose from her chair as quickly as her corset allowed. "We'll do no such thing. The Thorpe family will stay together. Delight won't leave this house."

Once again, Dr. Reeves ignored her. "What about the new women's college, Radcliffe, yes, Radcliffe, that's the ticket. I could use my connections to ensure your admission, perhaps as a scholarship student. Wouldn't you love college, Miss Thorpe? May I use your Christian name?"

"Yes."

Dr. Reeves nodded. "Thank you, my dear Delight. Imagine what a splendid life you'll lead, cotillions, teas, fetching frocks, all of Boston society in attendance."

A downcast Abby glanced sideways at the twins but said nothing.

Charles chuckled in agreement but frowned when his father added, "Think of all the suitors who'll buzz about you like drones around a queen bee. It's a capital idea."

The thought of leaving Bram House thrilled me, but I had a duty to my young aunt. I turned to her. "What do you think, Ziba?"

She answered with a scowl and then remembered herself. Her face glowed bright enough to put a flame to shame. "Gentleman, there's sherry in the drawing room, though Edgar might consider coffee. Girls, it's time to return to your homes. I'll have Mr. Greer attend to you. After all the excitement of the day, Delight dear, perhaps you should go to bed. Good night."

Chapter 13

Resurrection

My aunt trounced off with me at her heels.

"Ziba, I didn't want to make a scene at the table, but I'm not a child. Why must I go to my room? What about Edgar's—"

She sailed down the corridor at the speed of a clipper ship. "Edgar Reeves is a sot and a fool. Ignore him."

Despite her abrupt manner, I pressed my case. "How can I ignore him? Please, Ziba, consider Radcliffe. There'd be no expense since Dr. Reeves has offered to arrange it, and most importantly, I would be near you in Cambridge."

"No."

"But why not?"

The gaslight may have concealed her high color, but it could not disguise the anger in her voice. "Because I need you, you empty-headed twit. Don't think I didn't notice you making a spectacle of yourself in front of Charles. You acted like a common trollop. How dare you."

I stopped in my tracks, my head pounding like a drum. "Trollop? Me? Ziba, how can you say such a horrid thing?"

Ziba did not speak for a full minute. Her eyes filled with tears. "I'm sorry, Delight. The excitement and the wine loosened my tongue."

I could not accept her apology. "Ziba, you confuse me. You said you wished me to be a social success, yet you belittle me at every opportunity, and tonight, you humiliated me in front of everyone. What is this nonsense about Charles? He's simply a young man who has been kind to me."

Ziba took a deep breath and gifted me with an artificial smile. "I apologize for my words, but Dr. Reeves has already been too generous. I'm afraid Radcliffe will have to wait. Now, go to bed like the sweet angel you are, and we'll have no more of it tonight."

She threw open my bedroom door before she stormed down the corridor. I vowed we would talk in the morning.

Bride had closed the draperies, and the fireplace blazed, yet my bedchamber had an icy stillness to it. I removed my gown, overjoyed to be free from the corset, but Ziba's rebuke continued to sting. How dare she treat me like a sulky child? I could not understand her ire, but something besides her outburst bothered me. No matter how hard I tried to dismiss it, Edgar's ghostly tale remained in my thoughts. Perhaps the wine had gotten the better of him, yet I did not dismiss his words.

The faded pages of my Bible fluttered. I rose and closed the door against the draft. I moved back to the Good Book and glanced down at the open page. One verse caught my eye, the Book of Numbers, 19:11:

He that touches the dead body of any man shall be unclean seven days. He shall be purified on the third day and the seventh day and shall be clean; but if he be not purged on the third day and the seventh day, he shall not be clean. Everyone that touches the carcass of the person

of a man, if he should have died, and the other not have
been purified, has defiled the tabernacle of the Lord.

I closed the Bible, took Papa's compass from under my pillow, and clutched it to my bosom. It comforted me more than the Holy Word. I walked to the window and peered down into the courtyard. The moon's silvery face managed to reflect through the fog. I said a prayer for our guests' safe passage home and climbed into bed. After the excitement of the evening, sleep was a welcome respite.

The sound of keening soon penetrated my slumber. It started as a low murmur before growing into an unearthly wail. Most frightening of all, it came from inside my room. I heard the gentle footpad as it moved toward my bed, but I lay rigid, unable to face the visitor. Something stroked the contours of my face. Human warmth radiated from its touch, yet I couldn't open my eyes. I wanted to confront it, but fear prevented me from facing my intruder.

Without warning, the sobs became a howl of such power my heart stopped. Death hovered over me. I prayed Our Lord in Heaven would forgive my sins and welcome me into His bosom.

The shriek softened into a lamentation, then a whimper.

Soft footsteps padded away from the bed, and the door closed. After an eternity, I opened my eyes. Blood rushed to my head. I looked about the darkened room and saw nothing.

I leaped from the warmth of my bed and put one foot in front of the other to reach my bedroom door. Except for the dim glow of gaslights, darkness bathed the hallway. I moved down the corridor to Teddy's room. I'd always feared opening closed doors because of the horrors that might lie on the other side. Thankfully, I found the little dear fast asleep, surrounded by rag books, toy soldiers, and cloth dolls. A garish Jack in the Box sat in a gloomy corner, grinning through the darkness. I kissed the sleeping child's forehead and tiptoed to Ziba's bedchamber.

She slumbered away in a four-poster monstrosity of a bed. I turned back to the freezing corridor and returned to my room. My bed and sleep beckoned to me, but before I could climb in, a light flashing through the draperies stopped me. At first, I thought a moonbeam had gone astray until it flickered once more.

My hand shook as I pulled back the draperies and stared beyond the fog into the Garden. Two lanterns moved through the darkened cemetery. The medical students, most likely the Spunkers, must have been making mischief in the graveyard. Would the Lord forgive them for defiling the bodies of the dead, or me for not stopping them? How could I ignore my Christian duty? I had to reason with those misguided young men and prevent them from desecrating the graves. Their eternal salvation lay in the balance.

Papa's compass glittered on the étagère. I grabbed my talisman, pulled on my robe and slippers, and dashed out of the room. Armed with the compass and a kerosene lantern to light the way, I charged through the court. The night air nearly froze me, but I ignored it. I raced up the carriage house steps and pounded on the door until I heard Bride's voice.

"Who is at our door at this hour? What do you want?"

"Bride, it's Delight. Please let me in."

She opened the oak portal, and a blast of warm, sweet air caressed my face. Her eyes widened when she realized who her visitor was. "Miss, you scared the bejesus out of me, yes, you did. What the devil are you doing out at this time of night and in your nightgown at that? Have you gone daft? Come in before you freeze."

I shook my head. "I can't. There are men in the Garden, the medical students, part of a secret society called the Spunkers. Please don't let my words shock you, but those vile young men steal bodies for medical dissection. I can stop them with Mr. Greer's assistance."

She crossed herself. "Medical students? Spunkers? Lord Jesus, miss, stay out of it. Go back to your room and forget about it."

How could a woman I had come to admire would refuse her Christian duty? "How can you say such a thing? They steal the dead from their coffins. We must stop them. Where is Mr. Greer?"

Bride shook her head. "He's gone to retrieve a body. I tell you, the young mistress won't like this business one bit."

My shoulders slumped at the mention of Ziba. "Yes, I know, Charles, uh, young Mr. Reeves, said this would disturb her. Bride, will you help me?"

She shook her head. "No, I won't go out there. Stay with me until my Prince comes back. We can't do nothing."

The warmth of the place seduced me. How I would have preferred to remain with Bride instead of traipsing through a graveyard in the dead of night.

"But we can. Bride, we must stop the Spunkers. They wouldn't dare molest two ladies, would they? I'm sure I can reason with them."

She refused to budge, and I realized words didn't have the power to change her mind. "Very well, I shall go alone."

Although she called out to me, I turned away and headed down the stairs. "Miss Thorpe, you come back right now. Miss Thorpe."

I ignored her protestations, bounded down the stairs, and dashed into the fog.

****

A few minutes later, I wandered around the darkened cemetery, stumbling in the slick grass. My teeth chattered from the bone-chilling cold, but I managed to call out to the villains. "Spunkers, I know you're here, and I know the evil you are doing. Please answer me before I call a constable."

Except for the cry of a distant whippoorwill, I heard nothing. Then a muffled voice cut through the silence followed by a burst of laughter. I moved toward the sound but lost my footing and fell. Light spilled over the moist earth, and I got to my feet. Another round of masculine laughter hastened my stride. I yelled out into the darkness. "I hear you. Answer me."

Someone sang out in waltz time. "One, two, three, one, two, three—"

The flare of a torch grew brighter and steadier as the chant grew louder.

"One, two, three, one, two, three, follow me, my sweetheart."

Another step and a vision stopped me in my tracks, and I knew it would remain in my memories until the day I died. An open casket of glass and fine mahogany lay on the edge of a grave. Riley held Mrs. Ellis Wentworth's elegant corpse in his arms, a gossamer shroud still covering her. He swung her stiff body in a slow dance. "One, two, three, one, two, three—how ravishing you are, my beauty."

He removed the veil from her face and then placed a passionate kiss on her dead lips. I gasped in shock. Riley glanced up, dropped the corpse, and lunged at me. I turned in flight, screaming out as I rushed through the darkened cemetery, screaming at the top of my lungs.

"Dear God, someone help me, murder! Murder!"

Riley chased me, cackling like a lunatic all the while. I sped into the darkness, barreling through the cemetery, running so fast that I feared my lungs would burst. I raced until I could run no more. Exhausted, I stopped to catch my breath and found myself standing in the center of a tiled sphere in an unfamiliar part of the garden. Greco-Roman statuary encircled me, and a pantheon of marble gods and goddesses stared down from an earthly Mount Olympus. I turned from statue to statue, my eyes searching for an escape. A snicker ruptured the solitude.

Riley jumped from the darkness onto an empty pedestal.

"You're a cunning beauty, Missy, better than the dead one."

Fiend that he was, he stood among the statues, grinning. "You ain't afraid of old Riley, are you, Missy? Well, if you ain't, you should be."

Thank the Lord, the fog lifted, revealing my path of escape. I broke into a blind run, racing toward the gate as fast as my legs allowed. My legs could barely carry me past the tombs and stone monuments to the dead. I stopped once again, fearing my heart would explode if I continued. The only sound I heard was my own gasping for breath. When I looked down at the grounds, the moonlight revealed the edge of an empty grave. Another step and I would have fallen in. I smelled the damp earth and trembled at the edge of the dark void that would soon be some poor soul's final resting place. "Dear God, help your poor servant."

All at once, a wraith charged out of the darkness and pushed me into the empty plot. The fall stunned me, but I recovered. I screamed into the night as I clawed at the earthen walls. "Help, in the name of God, help me. Please."

The moon lit sneering Riley's face when he peered down at me from the edge of the grave. "You think I'll get you out? No, not me. You're staying down there, you snobby bitch!"

He tossed a shovel full of dirt into the burial place. "I'll have you covered in no time. Won't nobody ever know where you are and it's evil good."

"Dearest God in Heaven, save me. Save me." I tore at the side of the grave trying to make a foothold while Riley shoveled in more dirt. "There's no escape for you, Missy. I'll dig you out after you're dead and have my way with you."

Before Riley threw in more earth, a man's gentle voice called out to the lunatic. "Riley! Don't hurt her!" Someone had answered my cry.

Edgar limped out of the darkness and pushed the drunken swine away from the pit. Riley swung the shovel and, in his gin-induced madness, nearly decapitated Edgar. "Almost got you, cripple."

Riley dropped the shovel before he ran off, laughing like a madman. Edgar leaned over the grave and pushed the tool down to me. "Grab the handle, Delight."

He grunted and strained using all his strength to resurrect me from a premature grave. I held fast as he pulled me upward inch by inch. His strength gave out with a sigh. Edgar dropped the shovel, and I fell back to the bottom of the grave. He called out down to me. "Push it back up, Delight. I won't drop it again."

I angled it up to Edgar, who took hold of the handle. Pressing upward, I prayed to the Lord Jesus that he would not drop me once more. Suddenly, I ascended from the pit in one smooth movement. Charles had joined Edgar at the end of the shovel.

The filth of the grave covered me, and I must have been a sight, but I could not contain my elation. Tears of gratitude streamed down my face as I threw my arms around my savior.

"Who did this to you, my darling?"

I could barely utter the monster's name. "Riley."

He grunted, picked me up, and carried me back to Bram House. Edgar limped behind us.

Chapter 14

Dr. Reeves

Ziba ministered to me, repeating the same question all the while. "What in God's name possessed you to go into the Garden, Delight? What?"

I remembered Charles's warning and said nothing. Ziba's face flushed an angry red at my silence, and I feared she might strike me. "Delight Thorpe, you are a wicked, wicked girl."

Bride washed away the dirt, and except for a few bruises, I felt unharmed. A half-hour later, Dr. Reeves, Edgar, and an anxious Charles entered my bedchamber. Dr. Reeves's greeting was brusque. "Good evening, ladies."

Ziba barely acknowledged him. "Thank you for venturing out this dreadful night, Dr. Reeves."

The climb from the grave had shredded my nightgown. Ziba selected a night chemise of delicate cotton and French lace, an immodest garment cut low enough to reveal the swell of my bosom. The moment the men entered, I pulled the comforter up to my shoulders.

Dr. Reeves placed his medical bag on the chamber table and removed his greatcoat. He wore a white linen shirt without a jacket, vest, or cravat. "Please forgive the shirtsleeves, I know it's unseemly, but I hadn't the time to dress. When I left Bram House, I had no idea that the rest of the evening would turn into something so, uh, stimulating. Luckily, Edgar reached me before I retired for the night."

Both Edgar and Charles were dressed in the same casual manner as their father. I could not stop myself from admiring Charles's strong forearms and broad shoulders. Edgar did not say a word. Ziba sat at the foot of my bed, her beautiful hair streaming past her waist, but Charles hardly noticed. From the moment he entered the room, his eyes never left me. The intensity of his gaze forced me to pull the counterpane up to my chin.

Dr. Reeves scrubbed his hands with carbolic soap while Ziba ranted away, not bothering to conceal her rage.

"It's all madness. Delight went into the Garden, and Riley attacked her. The mad dog would have killed her had it not been for Edgar and Charles. Now, the impudent monkey won't tell me what possessed her to go into there in the dead of night. When Charles brought her inside, she muttered some claptrap about a ghost awakening her, yes, a ghost. Such poppycock. Edgar should be ashamed for planting such rubbish in her head. I'll have Riley discharged in the morning, and that will be the end of it."

My words came halting at first, then suddenly tumbled out. "It wasn't a ghost. I saw lights from the cemetery reflected in my window. I thought the medical students were harming the graves. Perhaps if I reasoned with them, I might save them from eternal damnation."

Ziba directed her reply to Dr. Reeves instead of me. "Medical students? You thought medical students were prancing through the cemetery, disturbing graves. Who gave you that preposterous idea?"

I had to keep Charles's confidence even if it meant lying. "I've read about grave robbing."

The room went silent for a moment, but then I spoke again. "I've even heard mention of a secret society, the Spunkers Club, that pillaged fresh graves for anatomical specimens."

Ziba glanced from Charles to Dr. Reeves. "Say no more, Delight."

I ignored her and continued speaking. "I'm afraid I saw no students, just Riley. He stole poor Mrs. Wentworth from her coffin, danced with her, and then…kissed her dead lips. I'll never forget the sight."

Silence fell over the chamber once again. I thought Charles might speak, but he did not. Edgar appeared obsessed with his shoes, and Dr. Reeves twisted his mouth and then examined his hands. Only Ziba screamed in anger. "Almighty God in Heaven. My poor Delight, let your fears be at an end. I'll deal with that rascal in the morning."

Dr. Reeves turned on Ziba. "Rascal? You call that animal a rascal?"

Charles took his arm. "Father, please."

Dr. Reeves shoved his son away. "Be quiet, Charlie! Mrs. Thorpe, rascals are children who soap windows on All Hallows' Eve, not monsters who desecrate graves and attempt murder. I'll have Riley run out of town. When he came here, hat in hand, I warned the trustees of the cemetery not to engage him. He's the lowest scum from the docks, and yet, even knowing what he was, they still hired him."

One angry glance from Dr. Reeves had stilled Ziba's tongue. She glared at him, wide-eyed, but mute. The doctor opened his medical bag, removed a thermometer, and placed it in my mouth. Perhaps he knew about the Spunkers and their mischief and wished to ensure my silence on the subject.

"It's time to examine Miss Thorpe. I don't need an audience. Charles, please escort Mrs. Thorpe from the room."

Ziba's face colored. "He'll do no such thing. This is my house, and she is an innocent."

"Innocent?" Surely, propriety couldn't concern Ziba. A physician and gentleman such as Dr. Reeves would never do anything untoward.

The doctor's shoulders stiffened. He spoke in an icy voice, his back to Ziba and his sons. I read the contempt on his face. "Mrs. Thorpe, you called me here to care for your niece, and now you are upsetting her. Either you leave the room, or I will. We shall have words later."

Ziba glared when she returned his words. "Very well, Dr. Reeves, we'll speak when you finish. Good night, Delight. Come, Edgar and Charles."

I could not respond with a thermometer in my mouth. Edgar limped away, but Ziba hesitated for a moment, that is, until Charles ushered her out of the room and shut the door.

Dr. Reeves removed the thermometer, smiling with great warmth. "Well, there's no fever. Drink the laudanum, dear. It will help you sleep."

He placed a glass filled with bitter liquid to my lips. "Very good, my dear. Delight Thorpe, I must say you're a brave, but foolish girl. You should never have attempted to stop the medical students alone."

I heard the gentility and sweetness in his chiding and felt comforted by it. "So, you know about them too, Dr.

Reeves."

He nodded. "Yes, my dear. Every doctor in the city knows about the Spunkers Club. They have been around Boston for over a century and employ resurrection men like Riley to do their bidding. One seldom meets idealistic girls like you, with the mettle to stand up to them. How valiant you are, Delight Thorpe, but of course, I would expect no less from a Thorpe."

I shook my head. "No, Dr. Reeves. I'm not valiant, just silly and cowardly, but someone had to stop their evil deeds."

He extended his arms and helped me from the bed. "You're a brave girl."

I shut my eyes as he ran his hands over my legs and thighs. "You're a young Valkyrie. Your limbs are muscular, strong, and highly colored. My dear child, you should see the daughters of the rich, their skin as pale as fish bellies. They starve themselves in a constant battle with an intractable society."

In a nod to decorum, he pulled the gown over my legs, however, when I opened my eyes, I saw his face had turned a fierce crimson. "Those poor girls, forced to wear whalebone monstrosities to bed, their hands tied so the poor creatures can't escape from their ordeal. I've performed post-mortems on young women, their bodies deformed, and their livers bruised from wearing corsets. The rich not only torture the poor but even worse, they mistreat their own daughters. It sickens me, and I hate them for it."

His eyes burned with an intensity that frightened me.

"Is something wrong, Dr. Reeves? Have I angered you?" He shook his head and mumbled under his breath.

"No, my dear, not you." Dr. Reeves appeared to

calm down, but suddenly, his anger bubbled up once more. "Boston is a city of wastrels. They spend their lives in useless pursuits, drinking, gambling, and despoiling Irish maids while frittering away money they never earned."

I turned away, shocked by his manner and the fury that consumed him. Without warning, he seized me by the shoulders and held fast. The noble physician of a few moments before had completely disappeared. "Dr. Reeves, you're frightening me."

He saw my alarm and released me immediately. "Forgive me, dear girl, I beg you, forgive me. My anger at injustice often intrudes on my reason. Now we're alone, my sweet little puss, tell me about your mysterious ghost?"

Perhaps he would think I was a lunatic, yet I had to take a chance. "I spoke of it to Charles. You'll think I'm insane, but something came into my room that first night in Boston. It returned and woke me. When it touched me, I thought it was the end of me."

He did not say a word, and his face went as blank as a board. "Dr. Reeves, at first, I thought it might be a spirit in torment, but it touched me. I felt human warmth. Aren't specters from beyond supposed to be cold? If I hadn't been such a coward, I would have confronted it."

He gazed into my face for what seemed an eternity and then spoke with great sincerity. "Dear God, my poor child. I never believed in spirits, but I've seen things in this place that frighten even a rational man like me. Call them apparitions, call them ghosts, but they dwell here. Ziba will deny it, but a servant girl did go mad after she saw one of them."

His words pierced my heart like a sliver of ice. "Oh

Dr. Reeves, what a horror for the poor girl." The laudanum finally took effect. My pillow suddenly became quite inviting. "I beg to you forgive me, but I'm afraid I can't stay awake. Perhaps we can talk about it another time. I must bid you good night."

****

I had a vague recollection of the door opening just as I drifted off to sleep. I heard voices shouting, a man's laughter, a woman's sobs, and a slap, but in my state, I couldn't be sure.

The next morning, I awoke groggy from the previous night. Bride had left a tray next to my bed, an arrangement of leftover delicacies. I picked at the food and then managed to make my way to the window. The leaves from a red maple tree danced about the tombstones in the necropolis, but soon tired of the impromptu ballet.

I washed myself with warm water and changed from my bedclothes into a blue simple gown. A knock at the door brought me back to reality.

Abby, Clara, and Patsy entered, concern written across their sweet faces. They rushed toward the bed, their arms open in embrace, and encircled me. Clara spoke first, her lips quivering, her tears threatening to cascade down her cheeks.

"Mrs. Greer told us what happened last night. To think, while we were sleeping in the comfort of our beds, while you battled the odious Mr. Riley. Oh, the horror of it all, the sheer horror!"

She could not contain herself and sobbed uncontrollably. I sat up, plucked a handkerchief from atop the étagère, and dabbed away at her tears. "Don't worry, my dear friends, the Lord protected me. I'll be back to my old self in no time."

Abby's face became quite grave, her eyes cold behind her spectacles. "Delight Thorpe, you are now our sister. The girls and I promise to protect you as we do each other. We have decided to hunt for those horrible young men."

She appeared to be quite determined. "We'll join you in the burial ground when the Spunkers do their next midnight marauding."

The three embalming students placed their right hands on top of each other and then silently invited me to join them. Their resolve reminded me of the girls I'd lost in my village. I placed my palm on top of their hands.

"Abby, those words mean everything to me. My father always dreamed of a house filled with girlish laughter. How he would have loved to know I have such wondrous friends."

She smiled at the twins. "Perhaps he does know."

My chums stayed with me for an hour before Patsy proclaimed, "We have work to do in the basement." One final embrace and they left.

Despite my desire to leave Bram House, how could I abandon such wonderful girls? Rather than mope in my room all day, I tiptoed downstairs praying all the while Bride would not find me and order me back into bed.

Once outside, I took a deep breath of the fragrant pine and sumac that scented the air. Bride would have scolded me for leaving my room, but I wanted to post my letter to Miss Yates in Rachel's Pride. Just as I arrived at the gate, the walleyed messenger boy arrived, parcel in hand. "A package for you, Miss Thorpe."

I took the parcel, handed him my letter, dipped into my pocket, and found a nickel to reward him. At this rate, my generosity would send me to the poorhouse. He tipped his cap and rushed off. Unfortunately, I stepped into the entryway just as Edgar left the viewing parlor. He gazed at me in his strange way then spoke. "Hello, Delight."

Although I found his intensity off-putting, he had delivered me from a horrid, premature death, and I hoped he would answer the questions that gnawed at me all morning. How had he and Charles managed to change from formal suits into rough garments? What were they doing in the cemetery so late in the evening?

"Edgar, my friend, my savior. We must talk about last night before Mrs. Greer sees me and marches me back to bed. What were you doing in the Garden?"

He cleared his throat, hesitated for a moment, and then spoke. "I, uh, well, uh…good day, Miss Thorpe." And walked away. I knew he wanted to speak, yet for some reason, he couldn't.

Someone had written my name on the brown shop paper in a bold masculine hand. I opened the box and gasped at its contents, a flawless white orchid, pristine and beautiful. How had someone found such a treasure in wintry Boston? I found a note written on sandalwood paper in the same cursive on the package.

My Darling Delight,

Even orchids must bow to your beauty. It is my hope you will join me for Sunday services. Please be prepared at eight in the morning. I remain your friend and devoted servant.

Charles Reeves

I tiptoed into the empty scullery and found a warm spot to hide my treasure. I promised myself to cherish the exquisite gift until the last petal shriveled away.

Chapter 15

A Meeting of Souls

On Sunday morning, I paced the courtyard, awaiting Charles's coupe. For the first time since my arrival in Boston, I would attend church and could barely contain my excitement. I had taken special care with my appearance and had washed my hair the day before with a shampoo of soapwort root, glycerin, and lemon verbena Mrs. Greer had concocted. Bride rolled my locks with rags to curl them and then I dried my hair by the warmth of the scullery stove. Alas, I could not think of anything except Charles. I hoped he thought of me, at least a little.

I had left my room a few minutes earlier and noticed Ziba's chamber door remained shut. I assumed she was preparing herself for services.

Ziba appeared just as Charles guided his carriage into the courtyard. I had dressed in a stylish frock, a gown of hunter-green cashmere trimmed in black satin, but she wore a simple day dress without a bonnet or gloves.

"Ziba, why aren't you ready for church?"

She colored a bit and fixed her lips in a chilly pout. "Charles didn't invite me."

I had no idea Ziba wouldn't be joining us. "But that can't be. I thought the three of us were going together."

Before I could say another word, Charles jumped down from his vehicle.

Ziba grabbed me by the arm and marched me toward him. "Delight is still convalescing from her ordeal. I expect her back in four hours. Please don't tarry."

Charles cut quite a dashing figure in his church attire. She and Charles faced each other, but neither smiled.

"Dear Charles, I'm the Episcopalian in this family, not Delight. Perhaps in the future, I might receive an invitation to join you for Sunday service."

"I'll consider it, dear Ziba, I promise."

He flicked his horsewhip, and we were off.

****

I once read that the Greek demigod, Phaeton, drove his father's Chariot of the Sun with such reckless abandon that Zeus struck him dead with a lightning bolt. Surely those who watched as Charles's splendid two-seater hurled down Commonwealth Avenue swore the charioteer had been reborn. Charles whipped the horses forward, and we sped like the wind.

"I designed this vehicle to my specifications. Do you like it?"

"It's the most beautiful carriage I've ever seen."

He laughed when he flicked the horsewhip. "It should be, it cost a pretty penny."

The builders enameled the carriage black with stripes of wine and bronze and trimmed the black goatskin seats with walnut brown velvet. The mountings were bronze and copper. The builders had affixed gleaming crystal lamps and panes of finely etched glass that shielded us from the wind and dust of the road.

In the excitement of the morning, I had forgotten to

ask about my aunt. "Why didn't you invite Ziba to join us?"

Charles flicked the horsewhip. "I wanted to be alone with you without her hovering over us. She's a splendid girl, and I enjoy her company, but you and I never get a chance to talk when she's around. Besides, with two lasses, I'd have to engage a carriage. Father uses a driver on Sunday, but I don't." He had an impish grin on his face.

"I've been told young ladies enjoy racing. Is it true, Delight? Shall we see?"

I gave a nod, the carriage lurched, and we were off, twin stallions driving toward Tremont Street with Charles at the reins pushing the horses to their limit.

Trinity Church, a mountain of grayish-pink granite with rose-colored sandstone spires, loomed on the horizon like an empress, her magnificence ascending to the heavens. Our carriage halted in Art Square, an attendant tethered the frothing horses, and Charles helped me from the carriage after the exhilarating ride.

Stylish Episcopalians filled the square. The gentlemen wore morning coats while their ladies were arrayed in winter *toilettes.* Despite the freezing weather, everyone promenaded, moving at a glacial pace. The corsets and mermaid trains constrained the women. I had practiced the languid gait of women of quality with my embalming sisters. As Charles and I strolled among the worshipers, gentlemen and ladies alike turned to stare and whisper. Perhaps everyone noted that Charles Reeves escorted someone other than the beautiful Miss Wentworth.

As we entered the church, a celestial chorus of male voices rose in a glorious rendition of "Jesu, Joy of Man's

Desiring" accompanied by a massive pipe organ. The massive stained-glass windows bathed Trinity in prisms of unearthly brilliance. Charles directed me to the front pew, where Dr. Reeves and Edgar awaited us. Upon seeing me, Edgar's face reddened and he turned away. Charles placed his hand over mine where it remained throughout the service. Dr. Reeves smiled most graciously but never took his eyes off his eldest son.

After Mass, despite the cold, Charles pointed to a park in the distance.

"Father, I should like to show Delight the Public Gardens."

Dr. Reeves seemed taken aback at the suggestion, but then he smiled and nodded to his son. "Very well, Charles, if you must, but please don't overexert her. She's still my patient."

Charles and I joined the fine families as they promenaded toward the Public Gardens. When we reached our destination, Venus, the goddess of love, greeted us at the entrance. Of course, she was simply a statue, but I prayed it was a portent of the future. I was just a frivolous girl and a romantic fool, but I had reason to hope. Charles and I walked arm in arm, a gesture reserved for those who had come to an understanding.

We strolled through Camellia House, the great glass conservatory, open on the Sabbath and ablaze with crimsons, aquamarine, deep emerald-green, and the sunlight yellow of the flora. Exotic birds squawked from the moment we entered the glass structure, and I had to strain to hear Charles's gentle voice above the hubbub.

"This isn't the season to enjoy the Public Gardens. It's very gay in late spring and summer when we have the Swan Boats." He pulled out his pocket watch. "We should be off. Ziba will have my head if I don't return you soon, but I hoped we might have this moment together. I've thought a great deal about that night."

I finally had my opening to question him. "As have I. Charles, please tell me, what were you and Edgar doing in the Garden that horrible evening?"

He spoke with quiet earnestness. "We were awaiting the Spunkers. Edgar and I wanted to dissuade them from their evil plans, but they ran off before we could."

My relief must have been palpable. "You and Edgar saved my life."

He lost color and swallowed hard. "Delight, before I return you to Ziba, I swear to you there's no truth to Eddie's drunken ramblings."

I remembered Dr. Reeve's words. "But Charles, your father said he felt ghostly presences in Bram House. He said a servant girl had gone mad after encountering a specter."

His mouth tightened. "There are no such things as ghosts, my darling. After that business with Riley, any sane person forced to live in an embalming parlor would feel as you do. You mustn't worry. The police are searching for Riley, and Mrs. Wentworth is back in her resting place. Still, a girl like you shouldn't be in Bram House. I've spoken to Father about having you stay with us until we find you permanent lodgings. Once you leave that horrid place, you'll never return."

It seemed I would soon be free, but I owed a debt to Ziba. "Charles, please don't think I'm flippant, or ungrateful, but perhaps my leaving Bram House is premature. Yes, I fled that first night, but now Ziba depends on me, and I have marvelous new friends. Besides, if that ghost is poor Uncle Ephraim, he would never harm me."

My savior pulled me close. "Very well, we'll talk about it another time."

A puckish smile lit his face, and my heart nearly bounded from my chest. "Delight, Ziba told me you're a budding poetess. Would you honor me with a verse?"

The mention of poetry lightened my mood. The girls in my quilting circle used to recite the verses of Tennyson, Longfellow, Emerson, and Mr. Browning.

Still, another bard held the greatest sway with my group. "My own verse isn't special, but I know of a recluse who lives in Amherst. Most of her poems are unpublished, yet I set more store on those few words than on those in great volumes. She wears only white and refuses to accept visitors. Her rooms must hold a treasure trove of poetry, but she won't share them with her admirers. One day, I hope everyone will read her verses."

Safe in their alabaster chambers,
Untouched by morning and untouched by noon,
Sleep the meek members of the resurrection,
Rafter of satin and roof of stone.
Light laughs the breeze in her castle of sunshine;
Babbles the bee in a stolid ear;
Pipe the sweet birds in gorant cadence— Ah, what
sagacity perished here!

My face must have blazed crimson, for this was only the second time I had spouted poetry to a young man.

Charles finished the verse, his eyes glistening with tears.

Grand go the years in the crescent above them;
Worlds scoop their arcs, and firmaments row,
Diadems drop and Doges surrender,
Soundless as dots on a disk of snow.

Neither of us spoke. Tears welled in my eyes too, but for once, they were joyful. My new friend had glimpsed my soul. "Dearest Charles, you know the poetry of Miss Dickinson?"

His voice quivered. "I regard her as a kindred spirit. I once traveled to Amherst to see her myself, but a servant turned me away at her door."

Charles's gaze entrapped me, and I could not look away. I closed my eyes as his forefinger traced the outline of my lips. Charles kissed my forehead. I had hoped for more, but he pulled away. "Dear girl, there's so much to say, but I can't speak."

We made our way back to Art Square in silence. A tiny girl dressed in a simple woolen dress and threadbare cloak carried a basket of fragrant Parma violets. "Winter violets for your lady, sir?"

Charles tossed a coin into the girl's basket, picked a sprig of violets, and pinned the flowers to my cloak. "They'll wilt in shame at your beauty. I have another gift."

He dug into his vest pocket and pulled out an emerald ring that he held up to the light. "This is for you, my sweet girl. It belonged to my mother. I'm told it has no flaws, but of course, I know nothing of such things."

The stone gleamed with blinding radiance. "I can't accept such a gift."

He closed my hand in his. "I beg you, take this ring in friendship."

"But Charles, we've only just met."

He seemed confused. "But I feel as if we've known each other for an eternity. Let me speak to Father. Perhaps he'll make you his ward, and you'll live in peace at our home."

His words confused me, but I pulled off my glove and slipped the ring on my finger.

"I'll accept it, Charles."

He took my hands in his and kissed them. "Do you think of me sometimes, my dear little puss? You see, I dream of you every moment of the day. Meeting you has transformed my existence. You feel that too, don't you?"

He pulled me into a secluded alcove. "Please tell me, do you think of me sometimes."

"How could I not, Charles?"

My answer must have pleased him. His eyes sparkled as he took my arm. We trudged back to his carriage.

Chapter 16

Rapture

Upon our return to Bram House, Charles and I found Bride in the courtyard with Teddy huddled next to her, both still dressed in their Sunday best. Teddy darted in my direction while Bride provided animated instructions to a worker sliding blocks of ice down the basement chute. "You, be careful with that ice."

Charles pulled his watch from his vest pocket. "My dear, you are returned promptly, and thankfully, my head will continue to rest upon my shoulders. Now, I'll speak to you as Father would. He ordered that you curtail all physical exertion for the remainder of the day, eat a light supper, and take the sleeping draught he left for you before bedtime. I'll call on you tomorrow."

He hopped from the carriage, lifted me from the seat, jumped back into the coupe, and rolled out of the courtyard.

"Delight!" Teddy ran to me, arms outstretched, and buried his head in my skirt.

Bride chuckled at the sight. "Master Teddy, you'll be the death of me. Miss Thorpe, ain't you chipper? The young mistress said Mr. Reeves took you to church. Mr. Greer and me went to Mass and brought Teddy with us. The boy loves the pomp of the true faith."

I pointed to the fellow from the Roxbury Pond Ice

Company. "Why is he delivering ice at this time of year?"

She flashed a mischievous smile. "It's for the stiffs, miss. I wouldn't bother with the rascal, except he's willing to deliver on the Sabbath."

I could live in Bram House until the end of my days and never be comfortable with the thought of corpses in the basement set upon chunks of ice. "Oh, yes, of course."

Teddy caught sight of a northern cardinal landed on the branch of an elm tree. "Red bird." The feathered creature flapped his brilliant wings and flew off. Teddy tore off toward the garden. Bride charged after him, but her gown constrained her. "Come back here, you naughty boy."

I called to Bride as I dashed after the child. "I'll fetch him."

He bolted through the secret entrance, and I caught up with him by the cemetery gate watching the three neighborhood hellions at play.

The little girl spied Teddy and ambled over to him. "Hello, funny boy."

She giggled, spun around like a top then whizzed off after the older children. "Goodbye, funny boy."

Teddy watched the children dash away, his mouth quivering as if he might break into tears at any moment. "I'll play with you, Teddy. Run and hide."

He darted away from me with a laugh. I chased him past the gravestones, through the bleak paths, to the rear of the garden into a pine-scented glade. I saw a flash of crimson plumage through a cluster of oak trees. "Teddy, it's the red bird."

Teddy shrieked with joy and ran off like a shot

following the shock of scarlet behind a marble mausoleum. "Teddy? Teddy, where are you?"

I heard a childish giggle then Teddy jumped in front of me. "Surprise! Surprise!"

I feigned shock and embraced him. "Teddy, you're a naughty boy."

With warning, angry voices ruptured the quiet. Ziba stood, a golden-haired warrior, pointing her rifle at Riley's head. When had that swine entered the garden?

"Get out, or I'll kill you with this rifle. It belonged to my late father. It's loaded, and I'm a crack shot." He cackled like a madman and then rushed away.

I grabbed Teddy by the hand and hurried him away. "Teddy, we must go home."

We rushed down the path to Bram House, the silence of a Sunday afternoon surrounding us. Without warning, Riley emerged from nowhere, a vile grin plastered across his face. He doffed his greasy bowler and barred our way.

"Good morning, Miss Delight. All decked out like the Queen of Sheba with the little halfwit at her heels."

Teddy buried his head in my skirt. I pushed the child behind me, leaned down, and picked up a round stone.

"Mr. Riley, allow us to pass."

The scoundrel had the nerve to laugh. "To hell with all of you! That whore of an aunt of yours is up to her neck in this humbug. Little lady, you ain't seen the last of me. Will that lemon drop or the college boy protect you next time? Nah, I'll get you when you least expect it."

He walked backward in the direction of a mausoleum. "Think you're better than me, don't you? I can see it in your eyes. Just wait. I'll get you, Missy. I'll get you good."

Teddy ran from behind my skirt, picked up a rock, and tossed it with all the power he could muster. It landed at Riley's feet. When the vile man lunged at the child, I threw my stone with enough force to hit the villain squarely in the chest. He stumbled and fell to the ground.

"Mr. Riley, I won't tolerate you hurting Teddy, your use of profanity, nor your insults about my aunt. I warn you, stay away from me. Next time I'll aim for your head, and I assure you, I won't miss."

Teddy's hand in mine, we stormed back through the garden. I shook at the thought of Riley's actions and his words. He had almost killed me and unearthed the body of a woman of great wealth. Riley called Ziba a "whore," defaming her as only a man of his low moral character would; however, he left me with one nagging question. What did he mean by saying she was "up to her neck in it?" Then I remembered Charles had assured me that the authorities were searching for him, but no constable had ever taken my statement.

We rushed past the solitary mausoleum in the moat, with BRAM inscribed above the door. Teddy pulled his hand away and ran across the bridge into the tomb. Once again, I sped after him.

A gas chandelier illuminated the interior. Friezes of Roman warriors carved from the finest marble ornamented the walls while carved facades polished to a rich sheen adorned each crypt. My eyes soon grew accustomed to the dimness.

What I saw shocked me to my core.

Mr. Greer stood before a glass coffin, humming to himself as he brushed the jacket of the occupant. The deceased wore the dress uniform of a Union Army

Officer complete with fringed gloves and a sash across his chest. A Hardee hat festooned with a feathered band lay at his right side along with his saber. The body resembled a waxwork, pale, his fair hair and beard meticulously groomed.

Mr. Greer swiveled around at our approach and bent down to greet the child. "Hello, Master Teddy. Are you behaving yourself, my little sir?"

Teddy scurried over to Mr. Greer and bounded into his arms.

I pointed to the body. "Who on earth is that, Mr. Greer?"

He beamed at his handiwork. "It's Dr. Bram, dead these three months. Have you ever seen a nobler face? I had the honor of performing the embalming myself since your poor aunt couldn't bring herself to do it. I freshen him up every chance I get."

Mr. Greer held Teddy in one firm arm and locked the coffin with the other hand. He closed the velvet drapes that concealed the coffin, and pointed to another draped crypt, addressing me in his softly accented English. "Madame Bram rests over there. I take care of her too."

He must have noticed my revulsion. "You needn't be afraid of the dead, miss. It's the living who make trouble, not those who've passed on."

Perhaps it was time to broach the subject of my mysterious visitor. "Do you believe in ghosts, Mr. Greer?"

Mr. Greer regarded me for a long moment and shook his head. "Ghosts? I'm afraid I've become a proper Yankee. I don't believe in ghosts or spirits even though I come from Louisiana where they trust in spirits and taints." He paused for a moment as if in reflection.

"My owners bred me as a house slave. I was just a lad of fifteen when my master forced me to follow him to war. I'll never forget that terrible time, the dead, the heat, the flies and the maggots, the smell of a charnel house. My master died in battle, and I fled to the Federalists. Dr. Bram took me in, and that's when my life began. We left the Rebels to rot on the battlefield, but I searched for those who wore Union blue to bring them to the embalming tent."

The memories took over, and his eyes filled with tears. "One of the doctors died in battle, and no white man wanted to learn embalming. Dr. Bram said, 'Prince, it's time you had a trade,' and shared his skill with me. Times were cruel after the war, people were starving, but Dr. Bram brought me to Massachusetts and let me work for him. Now I stand before you, a Boston man."

He pulled out a kerchief and wiped his face. "Massachusetts is so different from Louisiana, most especially when the winter chills one to the bone and brume covers the city. The people here lack the *joie de vivre* of Louisiana, and I can't get gumbo except when my Bride cooks it. I've learned to read and write in English and live in a way I could never envision back home."

"Mr. Greer, Riley frightened Teddy and me in the garden today."

His skin flushed scarlet with rage, and he strode to the door. "The drunken sot, I'll get my pitchfork."

Chasing Riley would be fruitless. I barred his way. "I'm sure he has fled. The constable is after him, and Mrs. Thorpe threatened him with a rifle."

At the mention of an armed Ziba, Mr. Greer tossed

his head back and gave a hearty laugh. "I wager that coward ran all the way to Maine."

"Riley spoke in the most vulgar language, which of course, I can't repeat. He said Madame Thorpe was 'up to her neck in this humbug.' Those are the very words he used. Mr. Greer, what 'humbug'? Please tell me if you know. I give you my oath, on my dead mother's grave. I won't speak of it to another soul."

His laughter stopped. "Bride and I don't stick our noses where they don't belong. Colored people have to watch their step in Boston. Please excuse me, miss. I've work to do."

From his expression, I could tell Mr. Greer understood the meaning of Riley's words. Still, I didn't have the strength or the will to detain him. "I beg of you, please don't leave."

Mr. Greer walked away without turning back. He left me more confused than before I entered.

****

Just as Teddy and I ascended the Bram House steps, the walleyed delivery boy rolled his bicycle to the gate. He carried a bouquet wrapped in brown paper. "Greetings, miss. Although it's the Sabbath, I have a flower delivery for Bram House and a letter for you."

He followed me, bouquet in hand, and I directed him to the viewing parlor. "Please put them next to the rosewood coffin."

Teddy chose that moment to dash off to the kitchen. I went after him, but the messenger's screams turned me around. "No, I ain't getting near that, no ma'am. Good day!"

The delivery boy raced out of the house. I entered the viewing salon and found Ziba picking roses from the floor. "That lily-livered dimwit, his employer will hear of this, and I don't care if it is the Sabbath."

She read aloud from the note the messenger dropped. "Put a rose in my beloved's sweet hand. Her favorite flower in life will be with her throughout eternity.' Very well." Ziba plucked a single bud from the bouquet and made for the coffin. Suddenly, a crash sounded, followed by a child's scream.

Bride called out from the foyer. "Madame, come quick. Teddy fell."

Ziba thrust the rosebud at me. "Here, place this in her hand."

"Whose hand?"

"The hand of the girl in the coffin, of course, you silly goose."

She scurried out of the viewing salon. I pricked my finger on a thorn, licked the blood away, and then moved to the casket where a comely girl rested. The corpse, a young girl of about seventeen, had been gowned in white satin, her hair coiffed in long ringlets. A white lace veil covered her face, and her glycerin crème-coated hands crossed over her chest. I found them cold to the touch, but after a deep breath, I managed to ease the rosebud into her stiff fingers.

Task accomplished, I turned to leave, but Edgar entered the room and stood near the coffin. He gazed down at the dead girl, a wistful expression on his face.

"Sometimes, in death, a young lady takes on a beauty she never possessed in life. She's lovely, but not nearly as beautiful as you."

I scrutinized his face. His eyes were windows to some private anguish that I could not fathom. When I stepped away, he gazed at me for a long moment then opened his portfolio.

"Delight, I must show you something, but you must swear you won't tell anyone. Do you swear?"

"Yes, I swear."

Edgar's hands shook as he removed several photographs. "I took these photographs in the days after you arrived at Bram House. The same irregularity occurred in every image, something hovering near the deceased."

I felt a sense of dread the moment he stopped speaking. "Edgar, if you have something for me, hand them to me now."

My skin crawled when I took the images from him and examined them. A face lurked behind each corpse, my dead uncle's visage, a serene smile on his lips.

Could Ephraim Thorpe be my ghost? My intellect railed against it, but my emotions thought differently.

"Edgar, we must show these to Ziba."

He blanched at the mention of her name. "No, no, Delight, no, but there is something I must tell you."

Before he uttered another word, Ziba called, "Delight. Delight. Where are you? You should be in bed!"

I looked down the corridor. "She's calling, and I must leave you." I turned back to him. "Edgar, you have my eternal thanks for saving my life. We'll talk later, dear friend, but now I must leave you."

I could feel his eyes on me as I rushed off.

****

That evening, I sat alone in my room, cocooned in my coverlet, and thought of the photograph with Uncle Ephraim's placid visage in the photograph. When I came to Boston, I hoped my dead uncle would be a distant memory. Unfortunately, the grave could not contain his tormented soul.

A rap at my door, and Bride entered, carrying a tray of hot bread, soup, and fruit compote. Although I had recovered from my injuries, she insisted on treating me like an invalid and remained solicitous about my welfare. After heating the mattress, she helped me with my evening ablutions. "Your bed is nice and toasty, miss. Madame ordered me to give you the draught Dr. Reeves left. It'll make you sleep like a babe."

I consumed the magical potion and climbed into bed. A paraffin lamp bathed the chamber in warm amber. Without warning, Bride kissed my cheek, and we giggled like two schoolgirls. "Oh miss, you are truly the bravest young lady I've ever seen. It's time to say good night, dear girl."

"Good night, Bride."

Her kiss of friendship would make leaving Bram House even harder. The draught soon took effect, and my eyelids became leaden. I could not have fought off sleep even if I wished to. In my dreams, I returned home to Rachel's Pride and smelled the perfume of the forest and the scent of the sea.

A caw from a gull drew my eyes up to the sky. Plump clouds danced in the sky like dandelions through an azure field. I stood on a gilded widow's walk and fixed my sight on the azure sea. A whisper as faint as a chrysalis breaking free of a cocoon aroused me. Charles murmured my name and was at my side. He stroked my hair with a touch as soft as fine chamois. His voice vibrated against my ear.

"I love you, my darling girl. I'll never leave you."

He kissed me, at first gently as if brushing against a

cobweb. I felt his mouth on my throat and my shoulders, and I abandoned myself to the sensation of sweetness incarnate. Charles took my hand and led me from the widows' walk to the woods. He folded me into his arms, and we fell together onto the forest floor.

Chapter 17

The Embalming Girls

I opened my eyes, bewildered by my strange and wondrous fantasy. I could barely rouse myself in the room's bone-chilling cold and lay in bed, marveling at my wicked dream. I left my bed, wrapped Mama's shawl around my shoulders, and opened the Bible.

A locked garden is my sister, my bride, a locked garden, a sealed spring. Awake north wind, come on south wind, blow on my garden so its fragrance wafts away. Let my lover come to his garden and eat its luscious fruit.

It appeared that even the Good Book approved of my love. I felt emboldened for the first time since arriving here. I would look Uncle Ephraim's ghost straight in the eye if he visited me again.

Charles's beautiful ring glittered atop my ditty box. I promised myself that I would cherish it forever, and then went about the task of preparing for the day. Bride had cleaned and aired my tartan plaid gown. After I dressed, I made my way to the bottom of the stairwell. Hecuba sat in wait for me, ready to pounce. I glared at the evil-tempered feline, and she darted away.

The growling in my stomach directed me to the kitchen where I found a pot of oatmeal on the stove and water for tea. I was breakfasting in the pantry when Ziba entered.

"I've just received wonderful news. Mr. Clinton Russell Sr. is about to expire." I attempted a cheery smile but could not muster the strength. Ziba pursed her lips. "Don't worry, Mr. Greer will accompany us."

She took in my tartan gown and shook her head. "We'll depart as soon as you change into a more appropriate frock."

My shoulders slumped. One comment from Ziba and my new confidence abandoned me.

****

The hearse rushed up Boylston past Walnut, onto Chestnut, finally stopping in front of an oversized bowfront mansion on Myrtle Street. A swallow-faced retainer tethered the horses. Mr. Greer carried the supplies and followed Ziba up the marble stairs. She tugged at the bell pulley. I adjusted my black bonnet and then straightened the skirt of the ebony gown Ziba had insisted I wear.

A plump woman with a pronounced overbite and severe demeanor opened the door. Pince-nez spectacles covered pale eyes that disappeared into her face. I chided myself over my uncharitable thoughts, but in all honesty, the unfortunate housekeeper resembled an overfed rabbit. She scowled at the three of us and wrinkled her nose as if smelling something unpleasant.

"You're the embalming people, aren't you? The doctor is with him. He hasn't died yet."

A large court hall opened onto the main stairwell. Mr. Greer, Ziba, and I followed the housekeeper up the staircase. We entered the horror of a master bedroom, a dark, oppressive chamber made all the worse by the stench of imminent death.

A maid carrying an overflowing chamber pot hurried from the room. Dr. Reeves stood over an obese fellow who wheezed his last breaths. Upon our entrance, the good doctor glanced up but then turned back at his patient.

"Hello, Greer and Mrs. Thorpe. Delight, it's good to see you again. Allow me to introduce Mr. Clinton Russell, Harvard, Class of '42, a member in good standing of the illustrious Somerset Club, father, husband, and gentleman. Unfortunately, his health prevents Mr. Russell from being a gracious host."

The death rattle filled the room. Mr. Russell's time on earth would be short. Ziba placed a handkerchief to her nose. "How long has he been in this state?"

"Hours. I'm afraid he doesn't want to die. Perhaps you should wait downstairs."

Ziba glanced at Mr. Russell with a bright smile on her face. "His wife intends to purchase the most expensive coffin in Boston."

Dr. Reeves turned to us with a smirk, a dark aspect on his face. I stepped away from him. "Of course, she will, Mrs. Thorpe. It will be an opportunity for her to show off her wealth before the entire city. I'm sure the coffin will be the largest as well. I warned Mr. Russell that his girth would be the death of him, but he chose cream cakes and port over my advice. There's no reason for you to endure these noxious odors. I'll call you when he has expired so that Mr. Greer can start the embalming."

He turned to the grim housekeeper who stood in wait in the corridor with three housemen. "Ready the servants. It will take an army to transport him to the parlor. Cleansing him will be a most unpleasant task, and we'll leave that duty to the poor housemen. Mr. Greer, ladies, please wait in the parlor."

The housekeeper curtseyed and then glared at Mr. Greer with the face of an angry hare.

Ziba and Mr. Greer made their way down the enormous staircase, but I did not follow because I wanted to ask him about his offer to send me to Radcliffe. I approached the massive door that Ziba had left partially ajar. Dr. Reeves could not see me hovering outside it.

The doctor's voice stopped me before I entered the room. "Clinton Russell, because of you my valet awakened me from a sound sleep. I raced from my home in the dead of night to care for a fat troll who never did a lick of real work in his entire worthless life. You're like a drunken sot who refuses to leave the tavern. Everyone wants you dead, my friend. Your vile wife and wastrel son are anxious to spend your money, the embalmers wait downstairs to pickle your pathetic body, and the worms hunger to devour your remains. Farewell, Clinton Russell."

I heard a snort and then silence. I walked away, confused. Yes, I knew of Dr. Reeves's dislike of the rich of the city, but how could a man of such compassion harangue a dying man so cruelly? Mr. Russell was far beyond hearing his tirade, but the vitriolic words unnerved me. Surely, I had misunderstood the good doctor.

Ziba stood outside the parlor preparing the embalming instruments with Mr. Greer. Mrs. Clinton Russell, a grim matron, her hair styled in the sausage curls of the previous decade, sat on a chaise next to her son. Young Mr. Russell seemed little concerned about his father's imminent demise. "Mother, blast it, I made plans, and now I'll have to cancel them because of Father."

His mother eyed him coldly and hissed under her breath. "Your poor father lies on his deathbed, and you care nothing about him."

The young man ignored her words and turned his attention to me. He twisted his mouth into a lewd semblance of a grin, something I found disquieting under the circumstances. I bundled up the images of coffins Ziba had shown to the family. Mrs. Russell had selected a hand-carved coffin detailed in bronze that cost a king's ransom.

Ziba entered the room. "I think you will be well satisfied with your selection, Mrs. Russell. When Mr. Russell is finally put to rest and goes to his heavenly reward, he'll slumber in the style to which he is accustomed."

Some minutes later Dr. Reeves entered the parlor, dejected. "Mr. Russell has passed on. Now he belongs to the ages. He was a fine gentleman whom I considered a friend."

Mrs. Russell blew her nose and then turned to Dr. Reeves. "I know you did your best for my beloved husband. How shall I live without him?"

Dr. Reeves took Mrs. Russell's hand in his. "How will Boston live without him, ma'am? Dear lady, please know that he died valiantly and was comforted by your devotion."

I could not believe my ears.

****

Two hours later, Mr. Greer sat at the reins of the hearse. I recounted Dr. Reeves's words. "Dr. Reeves said terrible things to that poor man. He called him a fat troll, said he was worthless, and worst of all, that everyone wanted to see him dead."

Mr. Greer's back stiffened, yet he remained silent and stared at the road ahead.

Ziba dismissed my words with a cynical chuckle. "You must have misheard him, dear. Dr. Reeves would never say such things. It was a perfect embalming. Mr. Russell was an ideal client, still warm when we began our work. You have no idea how difficult it is to get a life-like appearance after two or more days. By that time, one often must fight blowflies. I'm thankful his servants washed him, aren't you, Mr. Greer? Without their help, he would have smelled like a rotting Clydesdale."

Must I listen to another conversation about the finer points of embalming? "Please, Ziba, speak of something else."

Ziba appeared peeved with me. "Dear girl, I simply wanted to add a little levity to this very sad occasion. Mr. Greer understands, don't you, Mr. Greer?"

He pushed the steeds harder with a flick of the horsewhip. "Miss, a jest or two lightens the mood when one works with the dead."

No matter how I tried, I could not understand her constant need to make jokes. "Ziba, an appreciation for humor may be essential for social success, but it appears your attempts at joviality are lost on me."

She answered me with a shrug of her shoulders. "Well, Miss Grumpy Face, there's nothing I can do if you persist in your belief in spirits and other such nonsense. I hope the séance clears up your issues."

Séance? "What séance?"

She cackled, the cynical edge to her laughter obvious. "Maggie Fox, the old fake, has been holding séances at Quincy House where Edgar has rooms. Dr. Reeves said it would be his honor to arrange one tomorrow night. He is convinced that Maggie Fox will end your fears."

My relief must have been obvious. "Papa held the Fox sisters in high regard. I know you think it's foolish, but I don't. Please, you must come with me."

She rolled her eyes and gave a small chortle. "Yes, of course, I'll go with you. There will be only one Fox sister. The other, Kate, is putting on her shim sham in England." Ziba gave a toss of her head and laughed.

"We'll bring the embalming girls too and I'll put on a better show than Maggie Fox ever could. I'll wear widow's weeds and cry buckets of tears, but I know that Maggie Fox is a fraud. She's a drunkard who makes her living by deception, and she won't take me in." Her demeanor softened. "It's time to go home, my Delight."

****

When we returned, Ziba approached the embalming girls and invited them to join us the next evening. The idea of a séance delighted them all, especially Clara. "Splendid, splendid. We'll dress in black for the occasion." She giggled. "Of course, we always dress in black."

The girls rushed off, chattering all the while about the proper attire for visiting specters from beyond.

Later that evening when we were alone, I finally approached Ziba about Edgar's image. "I promised myself I wouldn't alarm you, but yesterday, Edgar showed me a photograph of Uncle Ephraim's spirit."

Ziba's face turned as white as starch. The truth had tumbled from my lips, and I could not take it back.

She lost her composure. "I won't listen to your

nonsense. Edgar is a deluded drunk, and regardless of what anyone says, there are no such things as ghosts of the departed. Good night."

She turned to leave, but I stopped her with my words. "Ziba, there's one more thing we should discuss. Charles told me Dr. Reeves has invited me to live in his home."

Ziba turned to me, a nasty smirk on her face. "How kind of Dr. Reeves, but I'm afraid it will be unseemly."

She spun around and charged down the corridor with me following at her heels.

"Unseemly? Why is it unseemly?"

"A young girl living with three men? I won't countenance it. I took you in when you had no place to go, and now you want to abandon me?"

I tried to embrace her, but she pushed away from me and dashed into her bedchamber, slamming the door. I heard her sobs through the closed door.

I stumbled to my room. The events of the day had left me exhausted. I fell to my knees and cried my own tears of frustration. Yes, something had waited for me at Bram House, and I promised myself to confront it if it visited me again.

A ping on the glass interrupted my thoughts. It sounded like a prankster tossing pebbles onto my windowpane. Who would be outdoors in this icy weather? I peeked through the draperies.

Riley, lit by a shaft of moonlight, grinning like a madman, glanced up from the courtyard. I cried out in fright, closed the draperies, and rushed to Ziba's room.

"Riley is in the courtyard!"

Ziba reached for her robe, ran down the stairwell, pulled Dr. Bram's rifle down from the drawing room wall, and made for the courtyard.

"The drunken whoremonger."

I followed her out into the cold and found the court empty. Still, despite the inclement weather, Ziba and I searched everywhere. She screamed into the wind as she scoured the grounds. "I know who the real villain is, and after I shoot you, Riley, I will give him a piece of my mind!"

I did not understand her words, but her search proved futile. Thank the Lord Riley had deserted the garden. I dared not think what Ziba would have done if she had found the man. We returned to Bram House, and Ziba insisted on dosing me with laudanum. I slept like the dead.

Chapter 18

A Dreadful Mischief

By the time we reached Boylston Street the next evening, twilight had fallen. My stomach knotted at the thought of contact with an unhappy spirit, yet Bride's parting words emboldened me. "Miss, when the hobgoblin comes, spit in his eyes for me."

Dr. Reeves's driver had provided us with hand warmers filled with hot coals and fur-lined blankets to protect us against the wintry cold. The carriage smelled of embalmer's soap and radiated with nervous energy.

The thought of attending a séance animated Abby so much that she could not stop talking. "Although I don't believe in spirits, it's exciting to think there might be a ghost in Bram House. Just imagine and if anyone can summon it, Margaret Fox can. I know I sound like a flibbertigibbet, but I've never attended a séance before. Mrs. Hartley certainly didn't address one in *The Ladies Book of Etiquette*."

Clara and Patsy simpered in agreement, but Ziba remained grim, her disapproval obvious. "Delight, I know Dr. Reeves insisted on this silly hocus pocus, but it's just a waste of time. Maggie Fox, a medium indeed. She'll bamboozle you all with thrown voices and flickering lights."

I refused to let her sourness dampen the mood. "If

she's a fraud, we'll enjoy the show. Besides, since Dr. Reeves engaged her, you haven't lost a penny."

Abby nodded in agreement. "Madame Thorpe, please, this séance is the most exciting thing that has ever happened to any of us. As you requested, we dressed like widows. It's as if we were attending a fancy-dress ball."

Ziba puckered her lips. "Very well, enjoy yourself, though I will not. Regardless of Edgar's drunken rants, Bram House is ghost-free."

I understood my aunt's displeasure at the séance, yet I could not wait. We had all garbed ourselves in heavy widow's weeds against the freezing weather and veiled our faces.

The cabman halted the carriage in front of Quincy House. A lamplighter fired the gas jets that illuminated the entrance to the massive granite structure. A blast from the Arctic greeted us at the opening of the carriage door. A houseman, bundled against the freezing weather, helped us from the hack.

The huge doors opened, and Edgar stood at the entryway, a grim expression on his beautiful face. "Good evening, ladies. Margaret Fox is eager to begin."

We walked into the overheated lobby, an oven of goodwill, strong drink, and tobacco smoke. A boisterous group of Harvard students, intoxicated from rum punch and puffing on cigars, sang a raucous ditty.

Come, old friend! Sit down and listen!
From the pitcher, placed between us,
How the waters laugh and glisten
In the head of old Silenus!

I recognized the young men from Mrs. Wentworth's wake. The fellows had behaved like gentlemen during the viewing, but that evening, they had consumed substantial quantities of port and buttered rum. The tipsy young men joshed, guffawed, and belched like common hooligans.

Warmth came to my face when I saw Charles. He was resplendent in a gray waistcoat, standing at the foot of the main stairwell. He moved toward us, but one of the students, his face red from drink, staggered toward him. "Charlie, join us."

Charles greeted the young drunk with great civility and patted him on the back. "Not tonight, my friend."

The rest of the drunken students ignored the glares of other guests and continued their unruly behavior. Their laughter stopped the moment they saw us. Five young widows, our faces veiled in black lace, stood at the threshold.

Abby tensed under the scrutiny of the young men, and I took her hand. When Clara and Patsy followed, the chatter silenced. When the girls lifted their chins and sailed by the youths, the boys' demeanor suddenly became sober. The young men doffed their hats at the five young women in black and cleared a path for us.

Edgar joined us and limped up the stairs to the third floor and down a gas-lit hall. We stopped before a heavy oak door, one I hoped would free me from my ghostly apparition forever. A somber Dr. Reeves opened the portal and spoke in a voice barely above a whisper.

"Please enter."

A stout woman of considerable age stood next to him. White-haired, cane in her hand, she acknowledged us with a bow and greeted us in the same solemn tones as Dr. Reeves. "Welcome. I am Mrs. Underhill, Margaret's elder sister. The shades of the netherworld shall reveal themselves presently. Join us."

Mrs. Underhill hushed us with a finger to her painted lips and then led us to a darkened sitting room. Abby spoke in a whisper. "Goodness, it's colder inside than outside."

Abby had not exaggerated. The dark chamber felt embedded in a block of frost, cold enough for icicles to hang from the walls. The only illumination consisted of two candles and a paraffin lamp resting on the mantel. Through the dim light, I made out a circular table surrounded by chairs and the outline of a large cabinet positioned against a wall. Burning incense could not mask the stench of gin, apprehension, and grief.

The paraffin lamp shone on a woman dressed in black, who stood in the center of the room. "My name is Margaret Fox."

I had once seen an engraving of the three Fox sisters, Kate, Margaret, and their much older sister, Leah, in their youth. Margaret's virginal beauty had abandoned her, and the comely young girl from the image no longer existed. Although she still appeared more youthful than her older sister, alcohol had coarsened her visage. Grief lined her once lovely face, and strands of gray shot through hennaed locks she had fashioned into a loose chignon. Most discomfiting of all, she had a disagreeable odor about her, perhaps from all the liquor she had consumed.

Margaret Fox's eyes, however, were arresting, deep, and unfathomable, as if she carried the woes of the dead on her narrow shoulders. They welled with tears, and she stared at me with such intensity I turned away from the misery trapped inside.

She fixed her gaze on Ziba. "My poor dear, Dr. Reeves informed me that you have recently been widowed, you, a mere child."

Ziba pulled back her veil, her lips twisted in a semblance of a smile. "Yes, ma'am, I wed at eighteen and became a widow within two short years."

Margaret Fox stroked Ziba's cheek. "I see great sadness in your face." Miss Fox's words confused me. No one in Boston had a jollier disposition than Ziba Thorpe. Perhaps in the dimness of the room, she imagined something that did not exist. The girls whispered among themselves. Miss Fox's eyes misted as if her pain imprisoned her.

Miss Fox paused, sighed heavily then continued speaking. "I'm well acquainted with grief, for I lost my one true love. Give me your hand, dear girl. The spirits of those who had passed on first visited me when I was a girl of fourteen."

Although I had begun to doubt her ability, drunk or sober, Miss Margaret Fox might possess the power to release whatever roamed Bram House. I could not restrain myself from addressing the medium, so I stepped in front of Ziba.

"Miss Fox, my uncle, Mrs. Thorpe's husband, passed away a short time ago, but I fear his soul doesn't rest."

Ziba gave a loud harrumph and then splotches of red appeared on her face, her upper lip twisted. Thankfully, Dr. Reeves took a firm grasp of her hand before she could make a scene. "Mrs. Thorpe needs your help."

Ziba glared at the good doctor and cleared her throat once again. The embalming girls and I exchanged confused glances. Ziba had never requested help and thought the idea of communicating with the dead ridiculous. Charles frowned in his father's direction.

Edgar ignored everyone. Only Dr. Reeves remained steadfast. "We fear something is keeping Ephraim Thorpe on this earthly plane. Will you lead him to his heavenly home?"

Miss Fox nodded to the doctor and then welcomed me with a most doleful expression. "May I ask your name, my dear?"

"Delight Thorpe."

She took my hand in her icy one. "How old are you, my dear child?"

"Seventeen. I'll turn eighteen in early August, ma'am."

Without warning, Miss Fox swayed and would have fallen to the floor if I had not caught her. Perhaps a half-emptied bottle of gin sitting on the mantel explained her woozy manner. She righted herself and stroked my hand.

"I could tell by your manner you were born under the sign of Leo, the lioness, sanguine, regal, and protective of the young."

Miss Fox pointed to a collection of implements atop the table. "The tools of our work. The tambourine allows the departed to reveal their presence, the spirit trumpet to hear their whispers, and a slate pencil along with a board to capture the writing from the beyond. Touch them, and you will see there's no trickery."

The embalming girls backed away from the table, and no one dared handle the tools. While Miss Fox sat in silence, eyes shut, Mrs. Underhill directed us to our seats at the circular table. She recited the Lord's Prayer as we sat ourselves.

Our Father, who art in heaven, Hallowed be thy name. Thy kingdom come, thy will be done on earth as in heaven. Give us this day our daily bread; and forgive us our debts, as we forgive our debtors.

I took a chair at Margaret Fox's right, and Ziba sat at her left.

And lead us not into temptation but deliver us from evil: For thine is the kingdom, and the power, and the glory, forever and ever. Amen.

Dr. Reeves positioned himself next to me, while Clara took the other chair next to him with Edgar to her right. Charles seated himself between Patsy and Abby, who had joined hands with Ziba. We sat together in the freezing void, the only warmth from our palms and fingers.

Mrs. Underhill called out into the dark chamber. "Welcome all. Angels and ministers of grace defend us, bring airs from heaven, and banish the blasts from hell. I shall call on God, my most powerful advisor for guidance. Are you here, Divine Father of Light? In the name of our Father in Heaven, I command the spirits of the netherworld to show themselves. Spirits, I call to you. Oh, the shadows are parting, the mist lifting—"

We sat in silence for at least five minutes before I heard a loud snap, followed by a crack. Suddenly, popping and loud knocks filled the room followed by the sound of keening.

Miss Fox's head fell backward as though some unseen entity had struck her. The trumpet moved a fraction of an inch to the left, then to the right. It rose from the table and remained suspended in midair. The table shifted and then tilted to the side. A phosphorescent mass oozed from Miss Fox's mouth. It glowed brilliant white and smelled like the air after a lightning storm.

Mrs. Underhill murmured, "Ectoplasm, the essence of the spirit world."

The tambourine jingled by its own power before it fell back to the table. Miss Fox's eyes rolled to the back of her head, a ghastly sight indeed. We sat in the frigid darkness as the minutes ticked by, listening without moving as Miss Fox gasped for air. After what seemed an eternity, a reedy voice spoke out from the spirit trumpet.

"Delight Thorpe, ye will remain with the dead forever, throughout eternity. Ye must walk the halls of Bram House with the spirits of the dead! Come, come, and join us."

Uncle Ephraim's handsome face emerged from the darkness, floated upward toward the ceiling, and disappeared as quickly as it had appeared. Miss Fox's body shuddered, and she pitched forward, her head hitting the table with a thud. We sat in silence until she roused herself, her face florid and sweaty. "Miss Thorpe, your uncle has given me a message from beyond the grave. I'm afraid it's for you, my dear. You must leave Boston immediately."

Dr. Reeves's breath was on my cheek, and he clasped my shoulder. "What portal to hell have we opened?"

I found the apparition of my uncle confusing. Except for a blush to his cheeks and blue eyes, the ghostly apparition was identical to the *carte de visite* Edgar had shown me earlier. I released Dr. Reeves's hand, jumped up from the chair, and grabbed the candle.

"I've seen this image before. It can't be a spirit."

I made my way to the imposing cabinet resting against the wall. Miss Fox screamed out. "No!"

Her protest came too late. I opened the cabinet door. The candle revealed a *Laterna Magica* propped on the shelf. "Perhaps I'm a mere country girl, but even in my village we used a magic lantern during temperance lectures."

I fiddled with the lens cap. Uncle Ephraim's face hovered once again in the darkness then disappeared.

Charles leaped from his chair. "I knew there'd be duplicity, but I did not expect it to be handled in such a clumsy manner." He glowered at Miss Fox. "Margaret Fox, you may have hornswoggled all of Boston with your balderdash, but you haven't deceived Miss Thorpe or me either."

Dr. Reeves rose from his chair. "Charles, sit down."

Charles gave a violent shake of the head. "No, Father." He scowled at Edgar who withered under his older brother's gaze. "Edgar, how could you do this? Such chicanery, such double-dealing, using a magic lantern show to frighten innocents?"

Miss Fox appeared so disoriented that I could not tell if it was a ruse or from consuming too much gin. "I don't know what has happened. I know nothing of magic lanterns."

Charles would have none of it. "Enough of your lies, Margaret Fox. You and your sister are confederates with—"

Dr. Reeves jumped up from his chair before Charles finished his sentence. Father and son faced each other in such a rage I feared they would come to blows. My shoulders slumped in disappointment. Ziba had been right about the Fox sisters, but why would they put on such an elaborate ruse?

Before I could question Miss Fox, Patsy screamed at the top of her lungs. Charles moved closer to his father, the menace in his eyes obvious. I interceded between father and son fray before the two came to blows. "Please, Charles, Dr. Reeves, this isn't the place for fisticuffs."

They backed away from each other. I placed a restraining hand on Dr. Reeves's arm. "Dr. Reeves, I'm sorry for your trouble and expense, but I'm afraid Miss Fox can't be of aid."

Mrs. Underhill poured a generous glass of gin and handed it to Miss Fox. "Maggie, drink this."

Miss Fox complied and gulped the contents down. A white mass lay on the table next to the slate. It must have been the ectoplasm, but curiously, in the light, it appeared quite harmless and resembled salt-water taffy.

Ziba's beautiful mouth stretched in a wide grin as she marched up to Dr. Reeves, her hand extended. "Dear Dr. Reeves, I'm sure I speak for Delight as well, thank you for everything. Sorry, you didn't get your money's worth, but it was an amusing show."

One glance into his face and I stepped back. His complexion went crimson, and from his expression, it appeared that he would have gladly thrashed Ziba within an inch of her life. The room went silent.

After a long moment, he smiled, his teeth shining white in the dim light. He took her hand in his. "Yes, of course, dear Ziba. I'm your servant."

He tossed a pile of gold coins onto the table. My last memories were of Mrs. Underhill comforting a hysterical Miss Fox, and Dr. Reeves's hands trembling uncontrollably as he poured himself a glass of port.

****

Ziba smirked the entire way back to Bram House, smug in the knowledge Margaret Fox had been proven to be a charlatan. "Girls, now you know the truth. The

Fox sisters practice flimflam, the worst sort of deception."

Abby's chortling turned into raucous laughter so infectious that the twins joined her. "To be honest, Madame Thorpe, she may be a mountebank, but I've never had such a marvelous time in my life."

Clara and Patsy giggled in agreement then Clara chimed in. "We loved it. I thought my bladder would burst from fright. It was splendid, better than the mischief on All Hallows' Eve. If I had money, I'd pay to see Margaret Fox and more of her shenanigans again."

Ziba's mouth twisted in an angry pout, and she said nothing. For once in her young life, she was the Old Sobersides.

Chapter 19

Awakening

November 25th,
Dearest Miss Yates,
*Your last letter left me elated. I thank the Lord you
are well and thriving. I am overjoyed to learn that the
influenza has abated and no more have died. Unless an
unforeseen catastrophe prevents me, I shall visit
Rachel's Pride in the spring. We will have much to
discuss.*

*I hope you enjoyed your Thanksgiving as much as I
did. Bram House smelled of spiced pumpkin and mulled
wine in celebration. The local butcher delivered a fine,
dressed turkey for our dinner, and Mrs. Greer outdid
herself with the trimmings. The Greers and the
embalming girls shared our table. Their presence made
the mood quite festive. Mr. Greer led us in prayer and
thanked The Lord for our bounty.*

*I am confused, dear lady. Although I would love to
attend college and better myself, Ziba has been most
generous with me and I wish to repay her. I also have
made a number of new friends here. There is much to
ponder.*

Your daughter in the Lord,
Delight

On the Friday after Thanksgiving, I made my way

to the kitchen and found Bride assembling brushes, rags and vinegar, weapons in preparation for battling the sub-parlor fireplace. Teddy, as usual, had attached himself to her skirts.

"I didn't expect you down so early, miss. Breakfast is ready, and there's hot water for tea. I smell snow in the air, so I'd stay inside if I was you."

"Where's Madame Thorpe?"

"In the basement, miss."

There would be no venturing downstairs for me. After breakfast, I riffled through my sheet music. I searched through the lively tunes, hunting for works fitting for waking corpses, and found none.

My hunt led me back to the sub-parlor where Bride, with Teddy at her side, attacked the hearth with her usual vigor. "Goodness, Bride, that fireplace will never survive your onslaught. I've looked high and low for my music. Could some of it be in here?"

She pointed to the rolltop desk. "Yes, miss. There are sheets of music in there." Bride continued warring with the hearth while I searched through the ornate desk. I found the music and my attention strayed. I ignored the stuffed animals scattered around the room and instead scrutinized the photographic images affixed to the walls. One portrait of a grave beauty holding a Springfield rifle intrigued me. She wore a natty shell jacket, a knee-length skirt flowing over pantaloons, and high button boots. A kepi cap sat atop her blonde locks. I recognized the uniform of the Boston 32nd All Volunteer Brigade.

"Was that lady Ziba's mother, Madame Bram? A Vivandier? How bold, how daring."

Bride stopped battling the grate, stood up, and walked toward me. "Yes, it's from the War of Rebellion.

Madame Bram left the young mistress with her kin and followed Dr. Bram onto the battlefield. I've heard tales about her exploits as a soldier, loading the cannons, and carrying water to the wounded. Madame Bram foraged for food, nursed the wounded, and worked in the embalming tent. My Prince swears she killed her share of Johnny Rebs, too."

Another image, an unnerving one, caught my attention. A young, bearded officer stood over the corpse of a soldier laid out on a wooden plank, an embalming pipe running through his neck and stomach. I pointed to the photograph. "Bride, was that gentleman Dr. Bram?"

Bride crossed herself. "Yes. He was a great gentleman, God bless his soul, the kindest, most generous man on earth. Took me in when my old mistress sacked me because her randy husband couldn't keep his hands to himself. I thank the Lord Jesus every night for putting that godly man in my life and curse the pneumonia that stole him away from us. This place ain't been the same since he died."

Another image caught my eye, a tintype so macabre I shivered, yet could not turn away from it. Four unsmiling men in Union Army uniforms posed in front of a military tent festooned with wreaths of holly as if decorated for Yuletide. A mixed-race youth, garbed in an embalmer's apron and forage cap, stood next to Dr. Bram, a corpse laid out on a table in front of them. Other caskets perched vertically on either side of the tent, each holding an officer in full military dress, hands folded across their chests. I picked up a magnifying glass and examined the photograph. "Bride, I've never seen anything like this."

She glanced at the photograph and shook her head.

"Few have, miss. The doctors called themselves the Prière de Terre Embalming Party, surgeons of the Federal Army. They embalmed the bodies of the soldiers they couldn't save and sent them home. Prière de Terre is in Louisiana where my Prince came from."

"The name means Earth's Prayer."

Bride pointed to each man. "They needed prayers in that hateful place. This doctor is young Dr. Reeves. The gentleman in the center is Dr. Bram, God bless his soul, Dr. Thorpe, your uncle. The young fellow over there is my Prince, eighteen years old and already an embalmer."

Young Dr. Reeves, dashing and elegant, posed with my late uncle Ephraim. My heart lurched when I fixed my gaze on the visage of my uncle, but then the blurred image of a man at the rear of the tent caught my eye. I noted something familiar in his stance, yet I could not make out his face even when I held the photograph against an oil lamp. When I placed the magnifying glass over the image, my heart pounded with such ferocity, that I feared it would beat out of my chest.

"Dear Lord in Heaven!"

Bride jumped at my words. "What's wrong, miss? If you don't mind me saying, you look as though you've seen the devil."

Yes, I had.

I stared at the *carte de visite*, peering into Riley's face. He could not have been over fifteen, yet he gazed back at me, a quizzical smile on his lips.

"Is that Riley? How could the horrid man have been in Louisiana with Dr. Bram? I thought he'd only recently been hired."

She snickered. "Where did you hear that, miss?"

"On the evening of my accident, Dr. Reeves chided

Ziba for allowing a ruffian from the docks near the house."

Bride collected her cleaning implements. "You must have misheard him, miss. The sot worked for the family for ten years until Dr. Bram gave him the boot. Dr. Reeves found him another position at Mount Auburn. After Dr. Bram passed, Dr. Reeves brought Riley to the Garden. Will you be needing anything else, miss?"

"Yes, please. Tell me why did Dr. Bram discharge Mr. Riley?"

She pushed Teddy out the door. "Teddy, go to the kitchen like a good boy and play with Hecuba."

Once Teddy scampered off, she turned to me. "It isn't fit for a Catholic to speak of it, miss, but I know you won't rest until you hear everything. Dr. Bram caught Riley interfering with the corpse of a young lady."

I gasped, remembering the horrible night when the fiend kissed Mrs. Wentworth's dead lips.

Bride continued recounting her horrible tale. "Dr. Bram went mad when he discovered what Riley had done. I had never seen him in such a state. He horsewhipped the brute and would have killed the varlet if my Prince hadn't stopped him. I've kept quiet about this long enough. Riley is a lout and a resurrection man. He digs up the dead and sells their bodies to the medical students. Everyone except for the three embalming girls knew about it. Now you know too."

With that, Bride threw back her shoulders and marched from the room.

****

Desiccated leaves of green ash and pin oak rustled on the ground outside one of the older mausoleums. Mr. Greer fumbled about in the darkness until his lantern

170

flared to reveal the interior of a mansion of the dead. I took in the dust-covered floors and walls, lonely marble crypts with tarnished faceplates in need of a polishing, no ghostly horror, only melancholy.

"There will be an interment on Friday, Miss Thorpe, so I must prepare this place."

I decided to be forthright. "Mrs. Greer told me about Riley and his doings in the garden. I found it quite a revelation. It appears that the devil cut Riley and the Spunkers from the same piece of cloth. Tell me, was Uncle Ephraim involved?"

Mr. Greer's face clouded at the mention of Ephraim. "Yes, miss, but not like them. Your poor uncle was weak and couldn't control his actions. He's dead now and can't hurt a living soul."

Mr. Greer slumped onto a granite bench. "Evil doers used him, miss." He spoke in a whisper. "There are things I don't talk about, but I'll show you. There'll be a burial in the garden this afternoon. If you're brave enough, meet me after the young mistress has retired for the night. We'll enter the garden together. We can't stop the Spunkers or call them out, for they are armed. The authorities won't listen, but you will see all."

I feared what I might see. "Very well, Mr. Greer, I'll meet you tonight at ten o'clock, and I'll ask the embalming girls to accompany us. Please prepare the hearse for them."

****

At ten that night, after Ziba had fallen asleep, Mr. Greer, Abby, Patsy, Clara, and I made our way down an ice-covered pathway to the south part of the garden. Despite my warmest cloak, the cold enveloped me and wintry fingers clutched my face. The girls whispered among themselves, and then Abby spoke for them. "This is the most thrilling adventure of our lives, even better than the séance."

"I hope it is because we can't turn back."

A lantern illuminated the walkway. Mr. Greer led us to a perch behind a large mausoleum. "Watch from here, ladies, and don't repeat what you see. As I told Miss Thorpe, the rascals carry pistols, so we can't intercede, but we can memorize the villains' faces."

Clara clasped her gloved hands together. "Splendid, Mr. Greer, splendid. No matter what, I know one day we will persevere over those criminals."

The whispering of young men punctured the frigid darkness. I heard the resonant baritone. Patsy gasped as we watched the grave robbers confirm our worst fears.

We watched as Charles directed Riley and the Spunkers to complete their vile task. "Riley, you and the boys dig here."

Two of the same well-mannered boys I had admired at the Wentworth viewing wielded their spades along with the detestable Riley. The other young men waited for their turn. Mr. Greer whispered, "The soil above a new grave is loose. It won't take long to retrieve the body."

The Spunkers arranged lanterns around the plot with the lanterns and spaded over the fresh soil at the head of the grave. They worked in relays, three at a time, cutting into the soil at the top of the plot, digging into the earth that had not yet frozen. In a quarter of an hour, the young men had uncovered the coffin, using their ropes to pull it upright. They pried open the casket, revealing the corpse of a delicate-faced fellow. The celebration began, and the students made a lark of digging up an interned body.

Charles led the jolly toast when they shared a bottle of rum. "To our deceased comrade."

Abby shook her head in disgust. "We embalmed that boy, a youth of sixteen who died four days ago of pneumonia. How could they be so cavalier?"

Mr. Greer spoke in a low whisper. "Madame Thorpe ordered the young ladies not to use arsenic. The poisonous embalming fluid posed a danger to those young villains who'll cut the body apart."

They slid a rope around the deceased boy's neck much like a nose and dragged the body from the coffin, laughing all the while. Charles examined the rouged visage of the youth. In the dim light, I saw a smile waltz across his lips. "He'll make a cracking specimen when we get him on the table. Let's get to work, lads."

I blanch at the thought of the next indignity. They stripped the dead youth of his clothing and threw his fine suit into the casket. Within ten minutes, they had finished their gruesome task, closed the coffin, and buried it in the cold earth. Without warning, another figure walked out of the darkness. "Smart work, my lads."

Clara gasped when the lantern light revealed Dr. Reeves. That vile man had orchestrated the diabolical escapade.

Dr. Reeves turned the corpse's face toward his.

"Excellent, boys. Take him off to the medical school."

Abby squeezed my hand and hissed, "The rotter!"

Charles and one of the Spunkers wrapped the body in a sheet and followed his father to the South Gate. The others jumped on waiting horses and shrieked with abandon as they rode off into the night.

Mr. Greer took my arm. "Have you seen enough,

Miss Thorpe?"

I nodded. "So, Charles works with the Spunkers. I thought he studied law."

Abby took my arm. "I'm afraid you're mistaken, Delight. Young Mr. Reeves studies medicine. He plans to follow his father in his work. Dr. Reeves teaches at the medical school."

How foolish I had been, but why should I be surprised? Charles had already lied about everything, including his course of study. My wide-eyed naiveté must have kept Charles and his father much amused.

I turned to my friends. "This has been a dreadful night, but an informative one."

The five of us trudged back to Bram House. Before Mr. Greer loaded the girls into the hearse, we held hands as I said an oath. "We must never reveal what we have seen, but we will stop those villains somehow."

Later, as I ascended the stairwell, I bid a silent farewell to Delight the Innocent and welcomed Delight the Warrior.

Chapter 20

Quincy House

The next morning while Ziba worked in the basement, I crept into her bedroom. Her journal sat on her étagère. I scooped it into my reticule without a moment's compunction. If I could not destroy my ghostly visitor, at least I would discover what she knew about the bizarre occurrences in the graveyard.

I dressed in a gown of claret velvet, swept up my hair, and dashed off a short missive.

November 27, 1880

Ziba,

It pains me that you did not confide in me. We will discuss everything upon my return.

Delight

Bride took my note without uttering a word. Armed with Father's compass, my guide to Boston, and Ziba's journal, I formulated my course of action. On the night of the séance, I learned Edgar kept rooms in the old hostelry, Quincy House. I would take a trolley to Brattle Street and demand Edgar tell me all.

I had braced myself for what I might find in Ziba's diary, but nothing prepared me for its contents. She wrote rapturously and in lurid detail of her wedding night two years before.

My darling Ephraim entered my bedchamber,

smiling, spouting poetry. He removed my night chemise and had his way with me—well, to be honest, I had my way with him, but we are married, so there is no sin. I think I shall love the carnal side of married life.

I wondered how a young girl could enjoy the affections of a man of thirty-five, but of course, there is no accounting for taste. She continued writing of her wedding night in lurid detail. I will not repeat the passages, except to say she enjoyed it immensely and her honeymoon even more. However, what had begun on a bright note soon changed for the worse.

Dear me, Ephraim ranted about the S……s again. He screamed for hours and then placed his head in my lap like a despondent child. I fear my dear husband is under the sway of Dr. Reeves and is too weak to break away. What am I to do?

I finally came to the passage about Uncle Ephraim's death. The revelation shocked me to my core. He died a suicide.

Guilt so consumed my darling Ephraim that he hung himself in the carriage house. He must have committed the act during the night. Mr. Greer cut him down. The scandal would have destroyed us. Thankfully, Dr. Reeves rushed to my side. He declared we must blame his death on a fall. Oh, the horror of it! My love is dead. Despite his misdeeds, I adored him. I read further.

Charles came as soon as he learned of Ephraim's death. Unfortunately, my grief turned to something else. He brushed away my tears with his lips and kissed me with great passion, his tongue inside my mouth, then he lifted me onto the bed. At that moment, I forgot I was in mourning. May the Lord forgive me. How weak we women are.

She became Charles's paramour after poor Uncle Ephraim died. Charles was a cad as well as a liar. I found the next entry written the night of my encounter with Riley most illuminating.

I pray to the Lord that my diary never falls into other hands. My actions have brought me shame. Although I can lie to others, I must be honest with myself. I detest the way Charles googles at Delight. I am much more beautiful, a great wit, a sophisticate, and a young woman of the means. Why does a penniless country girl hold Charles's heart in her hand? I know she does not love him, but I do not understand why he loves her. I hate being such a jealous wretch. My darling Delight might have died, and what would I have done?

I ignored her slight about my appearance and shielded the diary from the eyes of the other riders on the trolley. I read on and found the next entry the most difficult of all.

To my great shame, I have continued the contract between Dr. Reeves and Ephraim.

****

On my previous visit, night had cloaked Boylston Square's steeples and stone buildings in darkness. In the light of day, I found it more magnificent than my guidebook described. Quincy House, a handsome structure fashioned from fine Massachusetts granite, loomed in the distance.

I strode down Boylston Street, past Doolittle's City Tavern to Brattle Square. Without warning, the sound of drums and Irish flutes floated through the air. A funeral procession with drummers, Irish pipers, and mutes in black regalia moved in my direction. I watched as the cortege moved past.

At the rear, the embalmers, Hyde and McCarthy, marched to the beat of a mummer's drum. I doubted that they remembered me from Mrs. Wentworth's home, but they turned in my direction and doffed their hats in unison. A chill icier than a Maine winter crawled up my spine. I would never escape the images of death. The funeral party continued its rhythmic march down the street, and I trekked on to Quincy House.

Smiling college lads tipped their caps in my direction. I hurried past matrons haggling with greengrocers and booksellers hawking their wares. A faded flyer outside a candle shop caught my eye—*A Congregation of Spiritualists at Faneuil Hall Led by the Great Medium, Margaret Fox.* I wanted to scream, "Maggie Fox is a fraud and a charlatan," to everyone on the street, but I remained silent.

Quincy House stood opposite the majestic Brattle Square Church. I pulled my cloak tighter about my shoulders against the cold. Just as I stepped into the street, the sound of a fire siren pierced the air followed by the deafening rumble of horses' hooves. Four stallions, nostrils flaring, mouths frothing, raced at breakneck speed, pulling a gleaming fire pump.

Could it have been a portent of impending doom? Perhaps, but undeterred, I crossed the street and entered Quincy House anyway.

According to my guidebook, generations of travelers had lauded the place for its spaciousness and the beauty of its decor, the excellence of its cuisine, and the conviviality of its patrons. I passed through the hotel's portal and strolled from the cacophony of the street into the quiet of the lobby. Unlike my previous visit, except for an old porter dozing in a corner and two jolly fellows enjoying a bottle of brandy, the vast room lay deserted. By the light of day, I noted drops of grease and wine stained the gold and crimson carpet as well as the chair cushions. A gas chandelier and a few pieces of stylish furniture were the only nod to modernity.

A bespectacled man puttered behind the front desk. I approached him, imitating the haughty manner of a Beacon Hill matron. "My good sir, I am here to visit my brother, Mr. Edgar Reeves. Please give me his room number."

The clerk, obviously no gentleman, leered in a most disquieting way. "You'll find Mr. Reeves's *atelier* in Room 306." He leaned over the counter, a vile smirk on his face. "May I say you are the most fetching of his many sisters?"

I ignored his boorish comment and cheeky manner, crossed the lobby, and ascended the stairs. Gaslights bathed the brocade-covered walls in a phosphorescent glow, and violin music wafted down the hallway, lovely but doleful. I took a deep breath before I knocked on the door. I heard someone on the other side of the portal grunt and then stumble around the flat.

"Blast. Who is it?"

A rumpled and disarrayed Edgar opened the portal. His jaw dropped at the sight of me. His eyes burned especially bright, yet once again, I could not stop myself from admiring his dark beauty. Edgar swallowed hard, and his pale skin flushed.

"Delight. What are you doing here?"

Rather than demanding the information outright, I decided to play the coquette and wheedle it from him. I simpered and extended my hand.

"My dear Edgar, I'm so sorry to disturb you, especially while you are playing your violin. That piece was quite beautiful."

He appeared delighted by the compliment. "Thank you. It's a work of my composition. Do come in, please."

Two men in checkered suits sauntered down the hallway in our direction. They snickered and cast lewd glances as they passed. "I'm afraid it wouldn't be fitting, Edgar."

He opened the door wider. "Is it more fitting for you to remain in the corridor? Pray, come in." Edgar closed the door after me. I abandoned my usual somber demeanor, approximated a girlish titter, and opened it again.

"Dear Edgar, I decided to visit you on a whim. I told the gentleman at the desk that I was your sister. In my short time in Boston, I'm afraid I've become an accomplished liar. It seems an essential skill for survival here."

Edgar nodded as he pulled out a chair. "We're all actors and must play our parts, Delight. Please be seated. I can order refreshments if you wish."

I slid into the chair and tilted my head in what I hoped was a fetching pose. "No thank you, dear boy."

An awkward silence followed my nervous giggles, and his discomfort was obvious. "When I opened the door and saw you, I thought an angel stood at the threshold."

I whimpered, "Oh, Edgar," and then lowered my lashes as I had seen Ziba do. I knew nothing about playing the coquette, but flirting appeared to work. He stared at me with rapt attention. I giggled once more and then surveyed the place. Perhaps his digs had once been stylish, but I found them dingy and cluttered, the air fetid. A garish carpet covered the scarred floor, and the paisley wallpaper peeled in spots. The furnishings consisted of a table, two threadbare parlor chairs, and a chaise stuck in the corner. The only illumination, an oil lamp, sat in the middle of the messy table. I found it difficult to act the coquette in the face of such bleak surroundings, but I did my best.

A jumble of personal treasures sat on top of the mantel that was crowded with the writings of Mr. Darwin, Longfellow, Emerson, and Browning and volumes by Whitman and Poe. Except for several exquisite charcoal character studies affixed to the wall, the ambiance was miserable. One image amidst the clutter piqued my interest, an ambrotype of a dark-haired girl in a feathered bonnet. "My dear boy, I believe this lady is your mother."

Edgar caressed the portrait. "How did you know?"

I pried the image from his hands. "One only has to take note of her brow and eyes. There's a marked resemblance to you. The women in your family must be quite handsome, as are the men."

He colored slightly, and I congratulated myself on my successful attempt at flirtation. I perused the drawings affixed to the walls, taking in each line and curve. "Edgar, I'm as impressed with your talent as an artist as with your musical ability."

His violin rested on the cluttered table. A pitcher of hot water and a platter covered with the remnants of greasy food sat next to a half-empty glass with silvery dregs. I spied his sketchbook through the disarray and picked it up. "More drawings, Edgar?"

His face reddened, and he grabbed at the drawings.

"No, please, Delight!"

The pages fell open to a charcoal study of a voluptuous female model wearing only a brazen expression and a corset. She must have been one of the "sisters" the smirking desk clerk mentioned.

Edgar appeared on the verge of tears. "Delight, you must think me a complete scoundrel. I know the drawings are immoral, but I'm paid well for them."

I slammed the sketchbook shut. "I don't judge you, Edgar."

His shoulders dropped. "Others have. Father considers me a lout incapable of being a gentleman. He's said as much on many occasions. Charles echoes him."

I banished the flirt, and Miss Sobersides returned. "Edgar, I've come to speak to you about your father and your brother. I witnessed them purloining a corpse with the Spunkers."

He slapped his hand to his forehead as if clearing his thoughts. "I am so sorry, dear girl."

I plopped Ziba's diary onto the table. "This found its way into my hands. It is her journal and contains the totality of Ziba's thoughts and actions. I know about her involvement with Charles and fear he used her in an ungentlemanly way."

He slumped in his chair and did not move. I took his hand in mine. "I beseech you, Edgar, help me. My life has been frightful since I set foot in Boston. A mad gravedigger and disinterred corpse welcomed me to Bram House. You were in the Garden the night of my encounter with Riley. Charles said you and he wanted to dissuade the Spunkers from stealing bodies."

He turned to me, tears welling in his eyes. His words started haltingly then tumbled from his mouth. "No,

Charles and I were there to help them. Father ordered it. I sometimes work with Riley and the Spunkers, resurrecting the newly dead. Perhaps stealing corpses is the only vocation for a wretch like me."

I stroked his hand. "I know your father forced you into this lunacy. He authored that ridiculous tale of a girl buried alive, didn't he? I'm sure he was behind the ghostly images of Uncle Ephraim. Why? Why did he conspire with Margaret Fox for that ghastly magic lantern show?"

Tears rolled down his cheeks. "I'm so ashamed. Yes, the ghost story was Father's idea. He thought he could trick you with spirit photography. Can you forgive me?"

I did not blame this poor boy. "Yes, I forgive you, but I must discover why your father used such vile chicanery on me. If you know, please, tell me."

At that moment, I could not stop myself from sobbing in frustration.

Edgar stood and placed his arms around my shoulders. "Please don't cry, Delight. I can't abide your tears."

He kissed my hands, and I wrested them away. "No, Edgar, it's not seemly. You must control your ardor."

My sudden move knocked over a vial of the silvery gray crystals on the table. I touched the contents with my gloved finger and took in the silvery dregs at the bottom of the glass.

"Arsenic. What are you doing with this poison?" Now I understood the reason for his extreme pallor. "You're consuming arsenic? Are you mad? Of course, you are. All of Boston is mad."

He gave a wary shake of his head. "It is a sovereign

tonic if used with care."

"Arsenic is as poisonous as snake venom. Farm wives kill rats with it."

Edgar took my hands once more, but this time I did not pull them away. "Delight, if I can't secure a place in your heart, I want to die." His beautiful eyes filled with tears. "Perhaps I'm a wastrel. Father says I'm weak like Mother. I want to be a better man. I can be one for you. My dearest, you are in my dreams every night. I love you."

"You profess your love, yet you've allowed your father to torment me?"

He released my hands and averted his face. "Don't you understand? I'm powerless against him. Besides, if I had told you about Father and Charles, would you have listened?"

I had been blind to both men, perhaps deliberately so. "Maybe I wouldn't have, but I do now. You say you dream of me, but you won't answer my questions."

He hunched forward and turned his attention to an emerald-colored liqueur. I watched as he poured hot water over a lump of sugar in a slotted spoon he held over the glass. As the sugar water dripped into the glass, the contents turned milky green.

"You see how the absinthe changes. When it turns, it becomes the *louche* and is ready to drink."

I had read of absinthe, a pleasure that was forbidden in polite society. Edgar sipped from the glass and savored it. "At first when one drinks it, one sees strange and curious visions, but later, the most wondrous things."

I stood, resigned to the fact I would not get answers from him. It was time to take my leave. "Poor Edgar, I forgive you. Please, will you take my hand in friendship?"

Edgar placed a gentle kiss on it. My heart ached for this beautiful, weak boy. "I must go now. I'm determined to end this evil. Good day, Edgar."

I heard him weeping as I left the room.

****

I raced from Quincy House and engaged a waiting hack. "Do you know where the Harvard Medical School is?"

The driver chortled. "Yes, miss. It's on North Grove Street, a more dismal place you'll never see."

"Please take me there."

During the ride, I continued reading Ziba's journal. Her entries recounted the sordid details of her carnal escapades with Charles. I reread their carryings on that horrid evening in the garden when Riley nearly murdered me.

I should have remained with Delight, but Dr. Reeves assured me she would be well. When I slapped him for what happened to her, the villain laughed in my face. Charles carried me to my bedchamber. My anger disappeared when he nuzzled my neck. His lips and tongue touched the inside of my ear. Oh, what weak creatures we women are. I tried to pull away but could not. He smiled, and I knew he had won again. "Don't deny me, Ziba. My feelings are true. Can you not appreciate how deep my affection is for you?"

Ziba's words no longer had the power to shock me. The artless parson's daughter had vanished the moment I saw Charles with the Spunkers. When the carriage passed the banks of the Charles River, I knew we had reached our location. The cabman stopped the carriage and pointed to a dour three-story brick building, bordered by a row of naked elm trees and an expanse of mud flats leading down to the Charles River, the Harvard Medical School. He had not exaggerated its dreariness.

The drab exterior belied its illustrious reputation. "Is this the medical school, sir?"

"Yes, miss. I'm afraid it is. Grim, ain't it? The students joke that the building that houses the madhouse is better than this place."

Where were the ivy-covered domiciles and grand stone edifices? The cabman balked when I asked him to wait for me, but I waved a dollar bill under his nose as insurance. After he swore not to abandon me, he helped me from the carriage. Once inside the medical school, I realized the exterior merely preluded the institutional gloom within.

Dour portraits of bewigged or bearded men, all of whom seemed to glare in disapproval, covered the walls. Chemical smells mingled with those of mold and dampness. The stench traveled down from the second floor and lingered in the air. Students scurried through the corridors though some loitered in the halls between classes. Two nurses in white caps and starched gowns moved down the halls, ignoring the catcalls that followed them.

A young fellow stopped me when I reached the second floor. I recognized him from Mrs. Wentworth's fete and the evening of the séance. He possessed a smug, overconfident handsomeness, and ogled me as if he were selecting a piece of chocolate to nibble on.

"May I ask what you are doing here, miss?"

I decided to try a similar ruse to the one I used at the Quincy House. "Sir, I'm seeking Dr. Reeves, Dr. Morris

Reeves. I'm his niece."

"Dr. Reeves's niece? I don't know where he is presently, but he has a lecture in the anatomical theater within the hour. I'm sure he'll be overjoyed to see you. He must be the most devoted of uncles."

The young man bowed and pointed to the theater, and I walked in the direction he indicated. What a strange place, a theater without velvet curtains, set pieces, orchestra, or audience. Instead of footlights, gas jets illuminated the chamber. The leading man, a cadaver, hung suspended from a support harness, his face and body draped with linen cloth. I looked closer and noted that from the contours of the body, the leading man was female, a prima donna with a plum role in the anatomy drama.

I paused before strolling up to the podium and debated the wisdom of unveiling the specimen's face. All the while, I prayed my suspicions were wrong. I put my fears aside, pulled away the linen veil, and gazed into the embalmed visage of Mrs. Ellis Wentworth.

Chapter 21

Gathering Clouds

Wisps of vanilla-scented smoke curled around the ceiling. I turned just as Dr. Reeves strolled toward me.

"Ah, the delightful Miss Thorpe. How I wish you'd chosen another time for your visit. Young ladies, especially beautiful ones, must be vigilant around medical students, especially the louts like the Spunkers. They have fire in their loins and are a randy bunch."

He strolled in front of Mrs. Wentworth's corpse, a broad grin on his lips. "Lovely, isn't she? A superb specimen."

The suspended cadaver dangled before me, eyes closed, skin yellowed like parchment. "How can you jest about something so hideous?"

I heard the emptiness in Dr. Reeves's laughter. "Life is hideous, my sweet girl. Look around you. Death, destruction, and poverty lay in every corner of Boston."

"You, sir, are a rotter. Good day."

He blocked my exit when I turned to leave. His grin turned to a sneer. "How dare you, you stiff-necked little prig. How dare you shame me. I studied medicine to serve humanity, but poverty fettered my hands. When I wed, I gained wealth beyond my dreams. Unfortunately, I married a spineless, sniveling cow."

I had hoped for a glimpse of humanity. Instead, I

found a leering shell of a man. Dr. Reeves pointed to jars filled with preserved body parts. "My father-in-law's heart, or what masqueraded for one, is here among the organs of some of the great families of this city, all those pious hypocrites."

He whipped his head in my direction, a chilly smile on his face. "I do so envy Charles. Ziba is such a spirited girl. How I wish she'd found me desirable, but after her marriage to your uncle, youth won out I'm afraid. Of course, Charlie willingly obliged."

Ziba's descriptive passages left no doubt as to her relationship with Charles.

Dr. Reeves took another puff from his cigarillo. "Unfortunately, both my sons are besotted with you, dear Delight, but it simply won't do. Charles will marry Miss Wentworth, not an embalmer's daughter, nor a harp-playing country wench for that matter."

Bile came to my throat when I glanced once again at what was left of Mrs. Ellis Wentworth. "Please tell me how you can treat a woman you once called a friend with such disrespect."

His laugh rang hollow. "Friend? That worthless baggage was never a friend. Do you think I would have had her as a confidant? She scorned my family with that long patrician nose of hers, tolerated me only because of my late wife's money and because she hoped that Charles would redeem her Sapphic daughter."

I steeled my shoulders against his anger. "Yet, despite your hatred of her family, you wish Charles to marry Miss Wentworth?"

Dr. Reeves regarded me as if I were an imbecile. "Don't you understand anything, you bumpkin? I loathe the family, but not their money. I've made them all pay for what they did to me and my mother. I would have had Clinton Russell on the anatomy table, but he was too fat for the dissection trough."

I remembered his spiteful words to the helpless Mr. Russell. "Did you dispatch him?"

He grinned and puffed another smoky circle, savoring his smoke as much as the poison that had spewed from his mouth. "He bored me, and I finally tired of waiting for him to die. Of course, if you accuse me, no one will believe you."

Dr. Reeves's words shocked me as much as having ice water tossed in my face. "I understand now, sir. For all your tirades against the rich, you are worse than they are. You must have enjoyed frightening me."

He suddenly became somber. "I told Ziba not to allow you in Bram House, but she refused to listen. It became my mission to scare you back to your wretched village, but all my attempts made things worse, didn't they?"

I steeled my shoulders. "Yes, they have. I intend to remain in Boston if only to antagonize you." I took a step toward the stairwell then swiveled back to him. "You used my poor uncle and drove him to suicide because of his guilt."

Dr. Reeves grinned and took another puff of his cigarillo. "Ephraim was weak and allowed himself to be used. He took the path of a coward and dispatched himself. I had nothing to do with it."

At that moment, I would have jumped into the St. Charles River to get away from the dreadful man. "Once again, I bid you a good day, sir."

He stepped forward, took hold of my arm, and held fast. For the first time, I saw something akin to fear in his eyes. "Let me leave, Dr. Reeves. You've nothing to fear from me. You've involved Ziba in your evil scheme, and I can't go to the authorities. Rest assured I won't tell a soul."

Dr. Reeves released me and then puffed another smoke ring. "Very well, my haughty beauty, I'll take you at your word."

Had I been a man, I would have challenged him to a duel to the death. "For the last time, good day, sir."

"Good day to you, Miss Thorpe. What a stiff-necked little moralist you are. But then what else could I expect from a provincial parson's daughter?"

I ignored Dr. Reeves's final insult as I dashed from the theater. "Miss Delight Thorpe, you are an interfering little prig. I knew you'd be trouble from the moment I laid eyes on you."

When I rushed from the theater, and in my anger. I almost collided with Charles who stood at the entrance.

His lips tightened the moment he saw me. He took my arm and walked me to the stairwell. "A friend told me that a young girl asked for Father. What are you doing here? Did Mrs. Greer accompany you? You have no chaperone?"

How I wished to be a different sex at that moment. I would have gladly given him a sound sock to the jaw.

"Must we continue this charade, Charles? You've lied to me from the first. I saw you in the Garden with the Spunkers last night. You're no law student, you're a cad who robs graves for your father. Are you mad? You, of all people, must be aware this evil will entrap everyone."

A trio of medical students approached, and Charles, ever mindful of propriety, stepped away from me. The young men tipped their hats in my direction but then greeted him with salacious hoots. We did not speak until the fellows entered the anatomical theater.

"Charles Reeves, you're a liar and most likely the worst of those odious Spunkers." I pulled the emerald ring from my reticule. "I wish to return this."

Charles placed his hands behind his back and glared at me. The varlet had the cheek to be angry. "I gave it to you freely. Keep it. It belonged to my mother. She has no further need for it. I want you to have it."

The man infuriated me. "I've read Ziba's journal and know the true nature of your friendship with her. Was the ring meant as payment so you could use me as you used her?"

His face colored. "Don't say such a thing. I've known Ziba since childhood and have great affection for her. I swear, I didn't intend for it to happen. Father pushed me toward her. I know I acted in a manner unbecoming a gentleman."

"You behaved like a cur."

"I've begged her forgiveness, but you see, I love another."

We gazed at each other for a long moment. "I hope that you love Miss Wentworth. Your father will be pleased."

"No, not her. Father insists we marry and will disinherit me if we don't."

He took another step forward, but I moved away from him, the ring still in my hand. "Delight, it's you who holds my heart in her hands, only you."

I am sure my jaw dropped to the floor. "Did you say that I hold your heart in my hands? I've never encouraged you."

"I hoped with time you'd develop feelings for me."

At that moment I knew I could never love Charles Reeves. "Make things right with Ziba, marry her, and never plunder another grave."

When he turned his face away from me, I had my answer. "Very well, Charles, I must be off."

I tucked the ring back into my reticule and marched down the stairwell. For a moment, I toyed with the idea of tossing it away, but I must be practical. Maybe I could sell it in the future.

I rushed away as fast as my skirt allowed but Charles caught up with me and was at my side once more.

"I know you're angry because I lied. Yes, I'm a cad, but I'm not a monster, and neither are the Spunkers. We serve mankind. If you were to break your arm, who would you want to set it, a purveyor of snake oil or a doctor trained in anatomy? Cadavers are scarce, so we acquire them any way we can. The true sin is to waste a body. One day medicine will save humanity."

The sincerity of his words nearly took me in, but I could not forgive his callousness the night before. "And what of Ziba? For her sake, I vowed to keep silent when your father admitted to killing Ethan Clinton Russell. What of your poor brother forced to work with that beast, Riley? Will you save them too? I doubt it if you continue debasing them and bending to your father's will."

He grabbed me by the shoulders. "For all his faults, my father is a healer."

I wrenched away from him. "He admitted to putting Mr. Russell out of his misery simply because he was tired of awaiting the poor man's natural death. I'm sure there have been others in the past and there will be more in the future."

When I searched his face, I saw emptiness.

"Mr. Greer called you evil, but he was wrong. You're not evil, just weak. It's late, and I must return to Bram House. I bid you adieu, Mr. Reeves." I turned and strode off.

****

Upon my return to Bram House, I marched into the viewing room. The fragrance of evergreens and clove pomanders welcomed me. Ziba sat alone on the settee, quite fetching in a periwinkle blue gown. She must have expected a visit from Charles.

I handed her the diary. "This belongs to you."

She twisted her fan so tightly that I feared it would snap in two. Her face turned bright scarlet, and she rose from the settee. "You stole it. How could you, Delight?"

When I remembered her cutting remarks, my temper flared. "How could I not since you've lied to me at every turn? You even had the insolence to accuse me in the face of your moral turpitude. Why didn't you tell me you were Charles's concubine?"

The candor of the country mouse shocked her. "You dare speak to me in such a manner after I took you in, clothed, and fed you." She stepped away but then stormed back, her nostrils flaring like an angry bull. "You don't understand, but how could you? Ephraim tried his best, but I'm afraid we were both under Dr. Reeves's sway. My poor husband couldn't stand the guilt and hanged himself."

Her voice caught, and she stared at the floor. "Don't judge me too harshly, but I felt relief at his death and turned to Charles for comfort. Does that shock you?"

"Knowing what I know now, nothing shocks me. Despite claiming to care for me, and swearing that I was a sister to you, you stood by while Dr. Reeves and his minions frightened me out of my wits. Riley would have killed me had it not been for Edgar. Is there no end to your duplicity?"

Tears rolled down her cheeks, shaming me. Despite everything, I knew she had done her best to protect me. How could I judge her for wanting Charles since I once wanted him too?

"Ziba, I know what it is to feel desire."

We sat together in the stillness, the minutes ticking away. Although we faced one another, neither of us said a word. Finally, she spoke. "I'm so ashamed."

She burst into tears, and I took her into my arms.

Chapter 22

Yuletide

A bitter December followed a terrible November. We knew this kind of weather in Rachel's Pride, bone-chilling cold, icicles on mustaches, frozen hands and feet, runny noses and chilblains, tendrils frozen stiff as if starched. Nothing could keep Jack Frost at bay. Every time I ventured outside, an Arctic cold wafted through the frigid air and brushed against my cheeks. With each chilly kiss, I felt as if I had packed my face in ice.

The citizenry put on a jolly face against the frigid clime, and the city became awash in taffy pulls, Christmas tableaus, and skating parties. Rich and poor alike donned their gayest costumes, brightest capes, and pelerines. Snow cloaked the streets in white, and sleigh bells and evergreen wreaths festooned every carriage and wagon that drove through the streets.

Ziba's twenty-first birthday fell on the seventh day of the month. That afternoon we closed Bram House and celebrated. Bride baked a delightful Martha Washington cake in celebration, and small gifts littered the monstrous sideboard. Abby, the Greers, and of course, the twins, watched as Ziba opened each present.

"Oh, my goodness, Clara and Patsy, thank you for the lavender water. Mr. and Mrs. Greer, I shall use these beautiful handkerchiefs every day. Abby, I so appreciated the issue of 'Puck,' for I'm sure there are many wonderful jests that I'll share with you all."

She turned to me, her eyes misting. "My Delight, I have a special place in my heart for Mr. Browning, thank you for the book of his works."

My embalming chums gave poetry recitations from Mr. Longfellow's *The Song of Hiawatha* to entertain her.

As much as she smiled, Ziba could not conceal her unhappiness. That morning *The Boston Globe* had announced Charles's betrothal to Miss Drusilla Wentworth. Ziba had lost him forever.

****

The hard winter brought a bounty of death. One frigid morning, three constables carried a body into the basement. The leader, a red-faced fellow with muttonchop sideburns, took Mr. Greer aside. "The poor devil pickled himself in whiskey and fell asleep in the alleyway behind a tavern. We found him this morning, frozen solid, dead as a can of corned beef. God rest his soul. He must have fallen asleep. True, he died from whiskey, but in truth, soldier's heart killed him."

They called it "soldier's heart," but I never found the heart in it. Too many veterans of the War of the Rebellion, vacant, uncomprehending shells, stumbled on unsteady legs down the streets of every town in Massachusetts.

When Mr. Greer directed the constables to place the frozen body on an empty slab, the men could not help noticing Lazarus, the teaching skeleton. Lazarus's presence may have explained their hurried departure.

Mr. Greer gestured to us to take our places at the slab. We all focused on the new corpse, his face bloated from drink, lips blue from the cold, fingers curled in death. Ziba touched his frozen body.

"Ladies, I'm afraid you'll have to wait until he thaws out before we can do a proper job. I have bookkeeping to attend to, but I'm sure Abby and Mr. Greer can lead you through the lesson."

The girls nodded in agreement, and sans Ziba, we occupied ourselves preparing other clients.

Bride called down from the stairwell. "Lunch is served. I made pepper pot stew. I'll wager you've never tasted the like. It'll vanquish the cold."

We rushed up the stairwell and devoured the spicy brew. Fortified, we all descended the basement stairwell an hour later.

Patsy stopped dead in her tracks and crossed herself. We turned in shock. The thawed man sat up on the slab, his eyes wide open, his befuddled brain attempting to take in his situation. The five of us stood, immobile, like corpses ourselves. No one spoke except for the real Lazarus. "Lordie, this time I'm done in for sure."

With that, he fell back onto the slab. Mr. Greer rushed down the stairs, approached the frozen man, and felt his wrists and neck for a pulse. "Well, the poor fellow is dead now. It's a sad fact there's no one to claim him." I looked from Mr. Greer to the girls.

"Please hear me out, everyone. I know we've all seen the dreadful actions of the Spunkers, but in this case, it would be a sin indeed to waste the poor fellow's body. Those young doctors would gladly brave the cold to retrieve the poor sot. Let's embalm him with one of the solutions that doesn't utilize arsenic. I'll send a messenger to contact Charles Reeves."

The girls turned to each other in silence. My words took Mr. Greer aback. "Miss, you can't mean we'll give this man's body to the medical students?"

Abby looked deep into my face and then nodded in agreement. Finally, I found the words to speak. "Mr. Greer, after the horrible things Dr. Reeves and his sons have done, I understand your reluctance, but we must be practical. With no family to mourn him, his remains would rest in a lonely grave in Potters' Field, untended, and unloved. Perhaps in death, the fellow can be of some benefit to his fellow man. I'll speak to Madame Thorpe. I've thought long and hard about it. Maybe it would be advisable to make friends rather than enemies with the Spunkers."

The room went silent as everyone digested my words, and then Abby took a step forward. "I think it's a capital idea. Perhaps we can dissuade them from their misbegotten lives. An exchange of ideas. Perhaps, we should have them to tea."

Patsy nodded in agreement. "A gentlemen's tea. I understand they are all the rage."

Clara chimed in. "A splendid idea. We'll use our feminine charms to tame those fellows."

The girls broke out into laughter, Abby the loudest of all. "Image us as brazen hussies!"

Mr. Greer answered with a grudging, "Whatever you say, miss." He picked up a bar of embalming soap to prepare the man.

****

On Sunday, Edgar, Charles, and his Harvard classmates came to take tea at Bram House with the girls of the embalming class. The three serving girls carried in silver chafing dishes and gleaming bowls of steaming Lobster Newburg accompanied by chicken salad, crackers, and olives. We ended the festive tea with *petits fours,* and coffee jelly covered with whipped cream.

Ziba appeared to have exorcized Charles from her heart and played the coquette with every man in the room. The embalming students abandoned their traditional black and garbed themselves in their finest day gowns, Abby in bottle green *toilette* that showed off her fine figure. She sat between two young men who teased her mercilessly. Clara with her bright blue eyes and jolly disposition simpered sweetly, and three of the Spunkers appeared besotted. Feminine charms indeed.

Patsy's russet-colored gown brought out her grey eyes. She took her place next to the handsome youth I encountered at the medical school. The young man's smirk had abandoned his face, and he hung onto her every word despite her lisp. It appeared that he had become her slave.

"Well call ourselves morticians. It sounds quite professional, don't you think?"

The besotted young man nodded in agreement. "Yes, Miss Duffy, the word 'mortician' is more genteel than an undertaker or an embalmer."

Her lips spread into a coquettish smile.

My chums may not have been well educated, beautiful, or skilled in social graces, but within a short time, they had enchanted the Harvard bucks, and even Edgar joined in. The dining room was filled with girlish giggles and boyish laughter. I discovered these working lassies in their hand-me-down gowns were accomplished flirts. After the young men had consumed copious amounts of tea and Lobster Newburg, Mr. Greer regaled them with his wartime experiences.

"In Louisiana, the heat, blowflies, and other critters cleaned off the flesh of any corpse left in the field within a fortnight. Those dead Rebs would have made wonderful skeletons for you fellows."

The room broke out in applause. Ziba seemed to enjoy herself despite Charles's presence. When we finished lunch, she tapped her spoon on the side of her teacup and silenced the young fellows. "Gentleman, please join us downstairs. It's time to introduce you to the funerary arts."

The group moved to the stairwell, but before I could join them, Charles took my arm and pulled me aside. "Delight, thank you. Ziba told me it was your idea to bring the fellows to Bram House. It's difficult for them to meet young ladies who aren't horrified at the thought of dissection."

"You're most welcome, Charles. Now, if you'll excuse me, I'll join the others."

He held my shoulders. "I won't excuse you, Delight. Why do you rebuff me? Can't we mend our friendship?"

Before I turned from him, we exchanged a sad look of farewell. "We were never friends, Charles. Friends don't deceive each other and stand silent in the face of danger. Please excuse me now, I'm needed downstairs."

He let me pass, and Edgar, who had been waiting on the sidelines, took my arm. For a healer, I found Charles Reeves remarkably obtuse.

****

The second week in December, Mr. Greer wreathed every portal in the house with evergreen boughs laced with berries and dried fruit. A huge pine tree stood in the foyer decorated with pinecones, dried fruit, tin paper, berries, and grosgrain ribbons in festive colors. My bisque doll graced the top of the tree. A Yule log burned in the dining room fireplace, imbuing Bram House with the smell of cedar and cinnamon.

Ziba and I sat down at the dining table. Cold permeated Boston, and I thanked Our Lord for the warm fire and my shelter in Bram House. Bride entered with a robust lunch of Ziba's favorite dishes.

"Madame, I noticed you didn't eat none your breakfast and picked at dinner last night. If you don't mind me saying, you've been a bit peaked of late. This sausage pie will bring the color back to your cheeks or my name ain't Bride Greer."

She placed the hearty fare under Ziba's nose in anticipation of the luscious fragrance restoring her appetite. Ziba licked her lips and inhaled the savory aroma, but instead of eating, retched. I flew to her side with an empty bowl and caught the remains of her last meal.

Bride watched a humiliated Ziba flee the room. "If the last month wasn't enough. Jesus, Mary, and Joseph, I'll wager the young mistress is knocked up."

Bride and I pondered this latest catastrophe as we cleared the breakfast dishes. "Poor Mrs. Thorpe, in love with a no-good bastard and now with child. The thought of it makes me want to cry."

"Save your tears, Bride. All is not lost."

I rapped on Ziba's bedchamber door until my knuckles turned red. At first, she refused me entry, but I stood my ground. She finally opened the door, her eyes crimson. "Delight, I'm ruined, a fallen woman, the whore of Babylon. I knew all was lost when my monthly flow didn't come. What am I to do? Everyone in Boston will know of my disgrace. I'll be a pariah. Charles doesn't love me, and now he's engaged to Miss Drusilla Wentworth. I can't give birth to a bastard."

"Is there any possibility that Uncle Ephraim might have fathered the child?"

She paused for a moment. From her expression, it appeared she was calculating her nights of connubial bliss with Uncle Ephraim and her last monthly flow. She answered with an abrupt, "No."

Tears streamed down her face, and I felt powerless to do anything other than wipe them away. "Ziba, there are remedies, and herbs to bring on your monthlies. No one will judge you if you use them, but perhaps you'll want to keep this child. Ephraim died recently. No one need question the paternity."

Her laughter sounded hollow. "I'm sure every bluestocking on Patriot Street will guess that the baby isn't his. I'm ruined."

I'd already considered her situation. "You aren't ruined, Ziba. You're a respectable young widow. There won't be a question of paternity. There are such things as ten-month babies after all."

From her expression, I knew I had her ear. I paced about the room, formulating a plan. "Bride and the embalming girls can let slip that you were *enceinte* before my uncle's passing. No one will be the wiser."

She shook her head. "Charles won't want my baby."

After Charles's villainous behavior, I could barely believe her words. "Why do you give a fig about what Charles wants after his disgraceful treatment of you? You and your child are all that matter."

Ziba slumped on her bed, and her tears began anew. "He was so ardent, so romantic, so—"

I could not pummel sense into her in her condition. "Ziba, I don't want to hear about your lustful nights with Charles Reeves. Blast the lying rogue."

When Ziba averted her face in shame, I softened my voice. "As much as I distrust him, a child might be the most valuable gift you'll ever have from him."

She burst into tears once more. "My life is a calamity. Oh, what an awful world we women live in. Adversity besets me at every turn. How much more can a good Christian girl stand?"

Ziba continued crying until exhaustion carried her off into slumber. I left her side and strolled through Bram House. I checked every fireplace, turned down the gaslights, and then stole into the scullery to visit the orchid I had abandoned so long ago. The bloom had thrived in its warm home and had given birth to new flowerets. It may have been a gift from a lying rascal, but the bloom signaled a new beginning. I gave thanks.

Chapter 23

The Darkening Storm

Two days later, I sat in the courtyard behind the reins of the coupe waiting for Bride. I had planned to join her on a trek to Quincy Market, the North End's great Mecca of commerce. Mr. Greer had readied the carriage, and the geldings chomped at their bits in anticipation of a gambol.

"Be careful with the horses, miss. They're a spirited pair."

"I'll be careful, Mr. Greer. I've driven a carriage before, but not as fine as this one."

He took his leave, returning to his duties in the basement. I hoped Quincy Market would be a respite from the previous month's woes. The horses were eager, and we had a distance to travel. I draped a heavy blanket around my shoulders and prayed Bride wouldn't tarry much longer.

A movement at the side of the carriage caught me off guard, then I heard a voice dripping with oil and malice. "Hello, Little Missy."

Riley stepped forward, sporting a spanking new bowler, a stylish winter coat, wool trousers, and shiny boots. From the absence of his usual stench, I surmised that he had washed. With his stylish duds and clean-shaven face, he only needed a walking stick to be a dandy. His partnership with Dr. Reeves must have been a fruitful one. I tightened my hold on the horsewhip.

"Riley, what are you doing here?"

"I'm a free man. I go wherever I please."

He moved closer, but I stopped him with my words. "Come any nearer and you'll feel the whip across your face."

He guffawed like the swine he was. "Aw, I ain't afraid of a whip, and besides, this ain't a social visit. You disrespect me, me who's been wrestling with maggots and worms since I was twelve. Little Missy, you'll never be rid of Riley, no matter how hard you try. And that goes for the young mistress too."

He scurried away leaving me to fume. A few minutes later, Bride, unaware of my visitor, climbed into the coupe. She chattered away as she checked off the items we would need for the Yuletide. "Let's see. I'm low on cinnamon, mace, and loaves of sugar. Hmmm, almost forgot, I need raisins and ginger too." She turned away from her list and scrutinized my face. "Miss, is something wrong?"

I did not want to alarm her or dampen her spirits, especially as she prepared for Christmas. Yuletide had always been a time of gaiety in my village. "No, Bride, everything is wonderful." Still, seeing Riley unnerved me. I had not seen the detestable man in weeks, but today of all days, he had appeared.

Even after we arrived at Quincy Market, thoughts of the swine and his vile master, Dr. Reeves, consumed me. I hitched the horses to a post and followed Bride to the entrance. Every manner of evergreen adorned the columns and Grecian porticos. An ancient fiddler accompanied an old woman on a hammer dulcimer. A crowd circled them and enjoyed the festive tune as well as the antics of a juggler garbed in motley. Although my Yuletide spirit had vanished the moment I had set eyes on that odious man, Bride ignored my dark mood. She bubbled with mirth as she pressed through the throngs.

Sawdust and straw blanketed the floors, and beribboned wreaths, pomegranates, and bright red cranberries hung from every brightly painted booth. Goods of every description, Chinese silk, fine English cutlery, and silk fans from Belgium, filled the booths, yet I thought of Riley. I could swear the villainous Dr. Reeves had sent him. I vowed to strike him from my mind, but I could not erase the memory of the smirk on the blackguard's face.

Bride and I made our way to the butchers' stalls where freshly dressed geese, turkeys, and every manner of fowl hung from overhead hooks. Suckling pigs stared at us from beds of greens. I imagined Riley, swine that he was, lying next to them, an apple in his filthy mouth. Even picturing the beastly man as a hog didn't lighten my mood.

Baker's chocolate, cinnamon, nutmeg, and sundry varieties of spicy fragrances perfumed the air and lessened the stench of sweaty shoppers and damp woolens. Boston's hoi polloi elbowed anyone who got in their way, but no one could match Bride. She dragged me along and pushed through the mob. Perhaps she thought her good cheer would infect me. It didn't. Bride noticed my scowl.

"If you don't mind me saying, miss, you're about as gay as a wet rag, and I won't have it. There's everything under the sun here. I plan to spend every penny I've saved through the year to make this Christmas a merry one."

Indeed, it was the time to make merry. To the devil with Riley, Charles, and Dr. Reeves. We locked arms and maneuvered through the throng. Bride and I purchased every manner of trinket, pocket mirrors, and penny whistle then picked through the finer goods—silk shirts, lace garters, watch fobs, and ivory combs. The fragrance of gingerbread and mulled wine intoxicated me, and my rage fueled my extravagance. Bride's good humor infected me and chased Riley from my thoughts, at least for the hour. Being a spendthrift fed my soul.

As soon as we returned from our spree, I informed Ziba of Riley's visit. "The reprobate, the scoundrel! I'll alert the constable and have Riley's guts for garters."

The thought of Ziba wearing Riley's guts for garters amused me to no end. I managed a restful sleep with no ghostly intrusion.

****

The next morning, I bounded down the stairs and found Bride uncharacteristically silent as she prepared morning tea. "Bride, whatever is the matter?"

When she turned, I saw her red-rimmed eyes. "It's my mam. She's gravely ill, miss."

"My poor Bride, I'll pray for your mother. I know what it means to lose the one who gave you life."

Before I could give her a sisterly embrace, Mr. Greer entered. "The young mistress needs you, miss. A lady is at death's door. There's no one else to accompany her."

In God's truth, I had not planned to leave the warmth of Bram House on that grim day but as Bride said, Ziba needed me. Mr. Greer hitched the chestnut geldings to the physician's coupe, and within the hour, we were racing down Commonwealth Avenue on our way to

Beacon Hill. Despite the snow, Ziba drove like a demon, and I grasped her arm.

She shrugged my hand away. "I hated asking you, but the girls are occupied downstairs. This client is from a family of great wealth. The master of the house even bought a hand-carved mahogany casket in anticipation of his wife's death. It has been sitting in their drawing room for two weeks."

Ziba turned to me, her mouth set in a grim line. "We don't have the privilege of being both poor and virtuous. I have no husband, no family except for you, Teddy, and—my little one. There are mouths to feed, including your own, Miss Delight Stone Thorpe."

Ziba flicked the horse crop, and the geldings trudged to the Back Bay.

****

Had circumstances been different, I would have enjoyed my excursion to this home. The mistress had selected a Chinese décor, pale yellow silk on the walls, polished ebony woodwork. She had filled her home with the finest Asian art, and treasures from Cathay and Japan, so different from the garishness of the other Boston households I'd visited.

When we arrived, Ziba took me aside. "I've been told the deceased was a woman of impeccable pedigree who had made an advantageous marriage."

Unfortunately, we soon discovered what a monstrous bore the head of the house was. He viewed us with contempt and wrinkled his nose. "I don't believe in embalming, but her friends will expect a viewing, so do your best when she finally dies." He pointed to the coffin sitting in the drawing room. "I've spared no expense and bought that splendid casket. The doctor is with her now and has assured me her end is near. Make her beautiful."

I saw a slight tremble, but his stern demeanor returned. "You must excuse me."

He gave a curt nod and strode out of the parlor. Ziba rolled her eyes when he left the room.

"The ass. All his money hasn't bought him half a cent of manners."

"He must have loved her once, Ziba."

"Pooh. I'm sure he never loved her, just used her for his pleasure. He owned her, like the rest of his possessions. Even in death, he wants her to be beautiful to impress their friends." She walked toward the threshold and then turned back to me. "Delight, perhaps you should inform the attending doctor of our arrival."

"Very well."

A chambermaid escorted me up the stairs and pointed to her mistress's bedroom. I marched down the corridor, but then a voice from my recent past stopped me. Dr. Reeves spoke in sugary tones, yet his words were shocking.

"My pitiful darling, what are you, a beautiful lap dog for your churlish husband? You decorated his home and adorned his table, but now he's abandoned you. Had he brought me in earlier perhaps I could have cured you, but now I am powerless. I've given you enough morphine to end your agony, yet you refuse to die. What am I to do?"

I pushed into the room in time to see him pull a pillow from her face. I rushed over to the deceased's bed.

"No, Dr. Reeves, no!"

The poor woman lay in death, her green eyes open, mounds of hair flowing over her shoulders like an auburn river. She had retained her loveliness despite the consumption that had killed her and possessed an ethereal beauty even in death. Glass bottles holding the concoctions used to maintain her beauty were scattered throughout the bedchamber along with bottles of laudanum and medicaments. Although a servant had made a futile attempt to dispel the sick room odors with perfume, the nasty smell permeated the chamber.

I closed her eyes, but they fluttered open again. Dr. Reeves pulled a timepiece out of his pocket and placed his fingers on his patient's wrist.

"No pulse. It's ten forty-five. With luck, I'll be able to lunch at my club."

Ziba entered and stopped when she saw Dr. Reeves. She extended her hand in feigned cordiality. "Hello, Dr. Reeves. I had no idea you were the attending physician."

He gazed down at his patent. "Her husband brought me in too late to be of real assistance."

Ziba took a step to the deathbed. "It's been a while since we've seen each other. Has she expired?"

He had a dark smirk on his face. "Yes, she has, Mrs. Thorpe. You may begin your work now."

I retrieved the tools from downstairs. We began the embalming with a silent witness. Dr. Reeves crossed his arms and kept his gaze on me the entire time. The monster knew I could not call a constable and implicate Ziba in his dreadful business.

Since the deceased had been consumptive, as a precaution, we covered her face with a cloth soaked in carbolic acid. Ziba walked into the hallway and called out to one of the maids. "Get a strong girl to help you strip the bed. Burn her chemise and the bed linens. Make sure you mask your faces."

When Ziba and I finished, the dear lady was the most beautiful corpse in Boston.

****

In her determination to outrace the oncoming storm, Ziba pushed the steeds to their limit. We quarreled the entire time. "No, Delight, it can't be. Even a madman like Morris Reeves would not be so foolish to do such a thing."

"I tell you I saw him. I walked in just as he pulled the pillow from her face. Of course, he'll deny he did it, but I know what I saw. We must go to the medical school and demand they intervene."

"Do you think there is a doctor in Boston who hasn't hastened a dying patient's journey to the great beyond?" I heard the frustration in her voice.

"I'm sure your father would never have done such a thing." She did not respond and kept her eyes on the road. "We must tell the authorities."

Ziba gave another flick of the whip. "What authorities are you speaking of? The judges who lap at his heels or the city fathers who fawn over him? I'll have Charles speak to his father, and hopefully, our connection with him will be at an end."

The truth did not make the situation more palatable. Mr. Greer awaited us in the court and tended to the horses. Ziba alighted from the carriage and surveyed the pewter-colored sky. "There will be a snow tonight."

When we entered the house, she searched the parlor with her eyes as if fearing someone might overhear us.

"Delight, if you utter one word about what you saw, we'll feel the power of his wrath. Although you've barely glimpsed his anger, you know how vicious he can be. I'll ask the Greers to stay in the house tonight in the event we have an uninvited visitor."

We entered the drawing room and found Bride in the

arms of her hare-lipped cousin, both in tears. "Madame, the news is bad. My poor Mam's pneumonia has taken a turn for the worse. The rogue she married can't do nothing, him being a man and all. I must go and watch over her."

Bride had been as impenetrable as the Rock of Ages, but she sobbed like a child. "For the love of Jesus, Mistress, I've got to get to her before…before she dies. Prince will return by the morning's light, and I will return as soon as Mam is better—if she gets better. Please, Madame."

Ziba embraced the crying woman. "It would happen now. Of course, you must go. Please tell Mr. Greer to harness fresh horses and take the coupe. It will be faster."

An hour later, Bride, her cousin, and I walked into the courtyard. Mr. Greer awaited them in the buggy, reins in hand. Bride pulled a cluster of keys from her pocket and handed them to me. "I prepared dinner and locked every door. Prince shuttered the windows against the cold. It would take the strength of Hercules to break into Bram House. Would you be an angel and put Teddy to bed? A wee bit of brandy in his milk will make him sleep, darling child that he is. Dress him warm and please, miss, help him with his prayers."

Since my arrival, Bride never allowed me to lift a finger around Bram House. I felt honored by her trust. "Of course, I shall, Bride."

She turned to walk to the coupe, and I put a restraining hand on her shoulder. "Please give your dear mother my regards."

Bride smiled with such warmth that I gave a silent entreaty that her mother would live. "Why, thank you, Miss Delight Thorpe, I'll gladly pass on your words."

With that, she embraced me. "You'd better get in the house, miss. There's a snowstorm coming for sure. Please, look after my little one and the young mistress. If Mam survives the night, I'll be back as soon as her fever breaks. You're a brave one, miss, and don't forget it."

She took a seat next to the girl with the harelip, and they were off.

Chapter 24

Silent Snow

December 17, 1880
Dear Miss Wentworth,

Please allow me to introduce myself. My name is Delight Stone Thorpe, formerly of Rachel's Pride, Massachusetts, and niece by marriage to Mrs. Ziba Bram Thorpe. I visited your home on the sad occasion of your mother's death.

A matter of great urgency and delicacy has arisen concerning our mutual acquaintances, Dr. Morris Reeves and his son, Charles. Rather than delineating my concerns on paper, it is necessary to speak to you in person at your earliest convenience. Should you agree to meet, I will await your instructions. I beg you, please refrain from mentioning this missive to Dr. Reeves or Charles.

I remain your humble servant,
Delight Thorpe

I trudged to a waiting trolley and posted the letter. Ziba would no doubt be furious when she learned of my appeal to Miss Wentworth, yet I felt it imperative to expose Dr. Reeves's misdeeds to someone of prominence. When her grief no longer consumed her, the wealthy and powerful Miss Wentworth might set me on the proper path.

Ziba left Teddy to my ministrations. Lantern in hand, she walked around Bram House, turning down the gas and checking the locks on each door and window. Teddy and I joined her in the study when she pulled her father's rifle from the wall and loaded the chamber before placing it back.

"A bit of insurance against uninvited guests."

I readied Teddy for bed and, remembering Bride's words, gave him his sleeping draught of brandy, sugar, and hot milk. We knelt at his bedside together, and he clasped his little hands in prayer, while I invoked the generosity of Our Lord.

"Heavenly Father, protect this babe from demons who live in the darkness and malignant spirits damned for eternity to the black abyss. Embrace this innocent child. Should he die whilst he sleeps, I pray you embrace his soul in the warmth of your bosom."

This poor, afflicted child had touched my heart profoundly. As a reward for his sweetness and obedience, I let him keep Papa's compass. "This is a gift for you, dear boy. It belonged to my father, the best man I have ever known. You must promise that you'll never lose it."

He reached for the compass, wrapped the chain around his wrist, and climbed into bed. I kissed his forehead and left the room. Ziba marched down the hallway. We regarded each other for a moment then passed without speaking a word. I continued down the stairs, entered the viewing parlor, and blew out the candles that surrounded a tiny coffin. An infant Mr. Greer had prepared the previous day slept in her tiny coffin, a dead cherub with bow lips and cheeks like winter apples. She lay next to a rag doll that Teddy had placed in her coffin.

When I turned to leave, my lamp suddenly went dark. I jiggled the lantern. The flare caught and lit my way. I had just reached the stairs when, without warning, something brushed against my leg. I yelped, only to realize it was Hecuba. "Shoo! Shoo!"

The cat followed me despite my protestations, trailing me up the staircase, along the hallway, and into my bedchamber. Before I could stop her, Hecuba crawled beneath my bed. "Hecuba, you stubborn beast, come out." She refused to budge. Defeated, I closed the draperies, undressed for the night, then knelt in prayer.

"I entreat You, Dear Lord, to forgive my silence concerning Dr. Reeves's treatment of that defenseless lady. Please Lord, I beg you, soften Ziba's heart so she'll forgive my writing to Miss Wentworth. Please, Heavenly Father, make her understand I couldn't stand aside and do nothing."

The trials of the day had exhausted me. Sleep beckoned, and I turned down the wick on my lantern. Hecuba leaped onto the bed, mewed, and settled at my feet. I pulled the covers about me.

Despite my exhaustion, I found myself unable to sleep and lay thinking over the day's events. Then, I heard a gentle footfall. Breathy sighs penetrated the stillness. Through the half-darkness, I saw the doorknob turn. I jumped up, grabbed a chair, and rammed it against the portal. Whatever horror lurked outside my chamber knocked gently then pounded the door with the ferocity of a demon. The thought of what I would see still terrified me, but I doubted it was Ephraim's spirit. An icy calm embraced me. This entity could not be any worse than anything I had already encountered. I picked up my lantern, pulled the chair aside, and opened the door.

"In the name of Our Lord, Jesus Christ, show yourself." I lifted my lantern high.

Ziba stood before me, hair loosened to her waist, eyes wide open, a somnambulistic fury staring blindly as if in a trance. She awakened, and her sobs began. I guided her back to her bedchamber and poured her a dose of laudanum and sherry. My young aunt drank the mixture without resistance. "I walked in my sleep when I was a child. I thought I had grown out of it, but Charles told me I'd started again. Delight, my Delight, are you going to leave me? If Teddy were to die, who would I have?"

"Ziba, I've told you, I'll never leave you."

"I have nothing, Delight. My only real friends are those tragic souls we embalm, the old, the diseased, boys snuffed out before they sow their wild oats, and all the babies and the little children, so many babies. Charles doesn't love me. He doesn't love me."

The laudanum took effect, and her words slurred. "The stillborn are the lucky ones, for they will never have to walk through this vale of sorrow."

She stopped speaking, and I kissed her brow. "Dear Ziba, you have me, the Greers, Teddy, and the embalming girls. In time, you'll have a little angel to love you."

Ziba gazed into my face as if questioning my words, then dozed off to sleep.

I left the chamber. Despite the dim gaslight and lantern glow, I found the corridor almost impassable. The lamp went dark again, but after one jiggle, it sparked slightly, providing a faint glimmer. I vowed to change the wick when I had time and managed to maneuver through the darkness that enveloped me. When I reached the safety of my bedchamber, I gave thanks for my deliverance from the day's hellish events.

One foot followed the other as I dragged myself to the haven of my bed, but then I stopped. In the quiet of the night, I heard heavy breathing and smelled the musk of unwashed male desire and gin. I had a visitor, one I knew too well.

Riley stood before me in the half-light, grinning like a lunatic.

"This is grand, you bitch, just grand. Your fancy man tried to buy me off, but Dr. Reeves paid me more. I told you I'd get you, Missy. I'll kill you first, and after, I'll take your virtue."

He rushed headlong, heedless of my lantern, and I hit him squarely in the face with all my might. The blow had little effect on the drunken sot. We struggled, overturning the chamber table. "Strong little cockchafer, ain't you?"

I scrambled under the bed, grabbed the empty chamber pot, and hammered Riley until it cracked and broke. The impact stunned him for a moment, but he regained his balance and charged again at me, grunting like a wild boar. I swung my parlor chair and brought it down on his head, knocking the vile creature unconscious. My lantern lay on the floor. I picked it up, ran from the room, and sped down the corridor to Ziba's bedchamber, screaming at the top of my lungs all the while. "Wake up, Ziba! Please wake up!"

When I reached her, the laudanum had done its work. She hardly stirred. "Pooh, I'm sleepy. We'll discuss this matter in the morning."

There would be no rousing Ziba, so I flew from her chamber, down the hall. I reached the stairs just as Riley staggered from my room, still able to walk. The brute's skull must have been made of rock granite. A stream of blood trickled down one cheek, and although he had a smile on his face, it was not one of good cheer.

I ran down the stairwell into the foyer, to the front door, and pulled at it. It was then I remembered Bride had locked it from the inside. I searched my pocket for the keys. To my great horror, I discovered they must have tumbled from my robe during the struggle with the beast.

Riley lumbered down the stairs so I ran to the sub-parlor. The Springfield rifle gleamed from its place on the wall. I thought of Ziba and Teddy and marched back to the stairwell, rifle in hand. Riley stood in front of me, bloodied from our last encounter, blocking my way, unflinching even when I pointed the rifle at him.

"Stay where you are, Riley, or I'll shoot."

"Well, ain't you the little soldier."

He lunged. I pulled the trigger without a moment's hesitation. Riley learned that I had been one of the best shots in Rachel's Pride in the most unpleasant way possible. He fell to the floor, eyes open, his face contorted in shock, blood spurting from the bullet hole in his forehead.

I dragged myself back to the viewing salon and sat, the reloaded rifle across my lap. How could I explain away Riley's corpse at the foot of the stairs? I would tell the authorities the truth. Riley had entered the house, mad with lust, and I had killed him in defense of my virtue and my family. Still, locked inside Bram House, I could not notify the constable.

Would the ensuing scandal destroy Ziba's business? Dear Lord in Heaven, I had much to think about. Ziba would probably be of no use for the rest of the night. If only Mr. Greer were here. Before I searched for the house keys in the ruins of my room, I had to reason out my predicament.

The business with Riley had left me in a pickle. The thought of that animal stealing into Bram House hours before despite our precautions chilled me to my core. Surely, we would have discovered him, if only from his vile stench. Dr. Reeves had sent him to kill us, but how had he entered the house?

I heard a soft tread.

A shadow fell, and I realized the architect of all this horror stood behind me.

I rose but could not force myself to turn around. The parlor chair slid away. Dr. Reeves reached from behind and dropped a key down my bodice. He spoke in as calm and pleasant a voice as if he had just arrived for tea. "I discovered this skeleton key among Charles's belongings, a souvenir from his assignations with your sleepwalking aunt. He'd told me of poor Ziba's affliction. We both knew who your ghost was."

So, Charles was even more of a villain than I had first thought.

"Dr. Reeves, I'm not dressed to receive callers. I must ask you to leave."

His lips brushed against my ear. "I'm afraid that won't be possible, my dear. Besides, you are most charming in your night chemise, and the roses in your cheeks are quite captivating."

I kept my back to him as I considered the right moment to shoot him. His ramblings so preoccupied him that he did not notice when I cocked the rifle.

"I'm vexed with you, Miss Thorpe. My plan had worked like a well-oiled machine until you came along and meddled in matters that had nothing to do with you."

"Dr. Reeves, your 'well-oiled machine' will sputter and fail. It will be the ruin of everyone involved. The scandal will bring Harvard to its knees." I spoke with confidence I did not feel and prayed he could not hear the hesitation in my voice.

He greeted my words with empty laughter. "That will never happen. Still, I wish it hadn't ended this way, my dear. I promise you, your death will be a gentle one and the Spunkers will be delighted with such a lovely specimen."

I ignored his attempt to unnerve me and concentrated on how to take a clear shot. "How I wish your father had smothered you at birth, Miss Thorpe."

I could not stomach more of his vitriolic rubbish. I turned and hit him hard in the chest with the rifle butt. When he fell, I stepped back, pointed, and squeezed the trigger. Drat! The rifle jammed, and instead of a boom, I heard an empty click. He struggled to his feet ready to disarm me. I swung the weapon, hit him in the face, then put my knee in his groin. Dr. Reeves fell to the floor, writhing in agony while I rushed away, rifle in hand, to the basement stairwell.

Although pitch black surrounded me, I descended the dark stairwell, one step, another, and finally reached the freezing embalming room. My body slammed into one of the slabs, and I groped around in the darkness until I touched a box of sulfur matches. I struck one. When the match ignited, I found myself staring into the face of a recently embalmed child. When I averted my head, my eyes fell onto the massive storage cabinet at the rear of the room. If its shelves could accommodate a man's body, it could certainly hold me. The match burned out just as I climbed into the bottom drawer.

Dr. Reeves worked his way down the stairs, muttering to himself. "Puss? Puss? You're a naughty puss."

I managed to remain silent even when I felt something cold lying next to me.

His angry voice cut through the stillness. "I won't be bested by a mere child. Delight Thorpe, come out, come out, wherever you are. Where the blazes are you?"

He cursed to himself. I saw the flickering lantern through a crack. Thank the Lord he ignored the storage box. I lay atop a block of ice, clutching the matches and the rifle, praying it would not jam if I fired again. Would I freeze to death before he left the chamber? No, I heard his footsteps walking upstairs, just before I turned into a block of ice.

I lay on my side, managed to light another match, and found myself face-to-face with a wizened old man. My nightgown stuck to the ice, and I could not move. The match burned out. I lit another to no avail and heard the muted thumping of my heart. A glance at the old man's doleful visage strangely comforted me. One strong tug and I rolled away from the ancient cadaver. I had hoped to escape, but when I tried to open the drawer, the cold had frozen it tight. Metal rubbed against metal as I shoved and pushed against it. Once again, I pushed with all my might and once again, the shelf did not open. I prayed. "Release me, Heavenly Father."

On a final heave, the drawer rolled out, and I emerged from the grave like a spirit on Resurrection

Day.

My teeth chattered. I was soaked to the skin, but alive. I still held the rifle, but drat, the blackguard had taken my lantern, and I stumbled around the pitch-black chamber. My last match flared. The flame revealed a scalpel gleaming on one of the slabs. Another weapon might be useful in the event the rifle jammed again. I picked it up, careful not to cut myself, and mounted the stairs.

Despite the darkness surrounding me, I made my way up the basement steps to the hallway. I would have to mount the stairs to the second floor in the dark to recover the missing keys in the wreckage of my room. Riley's body lay at the foot of the staircase, his eyes open in shock. I stepped away, quaking at the prospect of another encounter with his master.

From my periphery, I made out a figure descending in the dim light.

Dr. Reeves made his way down the stairs, carrying the lantern in one hand, and holding a sleeping Teddy to his breast. "I couldn't rouse your aunt."

"Please, tell me you didn't hurt Ziba."

He laughed at my concern. "No, I need the little fool, but not the child. I'd hoped to have one specimen for dissection, but since you dispatched Riley with ease, I'll have two, and soon one more."

His cruelty knew no limits.

"Dr. Reeves, please let him go. Do what you wish with me but leave Teddy. He's an innocent who understands so little. I beg you, put him back in his bed, and I'll go with you. I swear on my mother's grave, I'll do as you wish. Please."

I heard no madness in his voice nor saw malice on

his face. "My dear, put down the rifle."

I placed my weapon on the floor. "Please, Dr. Reeves, give Teddy to me."

The vile man spoke in a voice of icy serenity. "Bram should have rid society of this worthless child at birth. Now, however, he'll have a purpose in the world of medicine. Did you know resurrection men are paid by the inch for a child's body?"

He placed his hand over Teddy's face. The boy struggled for a moment and then went limp. The beast killed my darling Teddy! I screamed like a banshee.

"Monster!"

The scalpel leapt from my pocket. I saw the veins in Dr. Reeves's neck pulsate and without a moment's hesitation, slashed his neck, cutting his jugular and windpipe.

Blood spurted, spraying the wall in scarlet waves with each beat of his heart. He gaped in horror, dropped Teddy, and grabbed at his throat, silent except for a gurgling sound. I read the shock and fear on his face along with the unasked question. *"What have you done? What have you done to me?"*

He dropped the lantern when he staggered to the kitchen. Teddy lay on the floor, motionless, his eyes closed, Father's compass tangling in his hand. I knelt next to him, sobbing, cradling his limp frame in my arms. "No, no, no!"

How helpless I had been, unable to protect this dear child from that demon. I thought of using the scalpel on myself, but before I could damn my soul for all eternity, I heard a whimper. The tiny body moved. Teddy's eyes fluttered open, and he giggled. "Surprise."

I held him close to me, my tears almost blinding me.

"How naughty you are, dear Teddy."

He smiled at his deception then sleep overtook him.

A dark form appeared at the stairwell, Ziba, a dazed expression on her face. "Who made that frightful noise?" She bent down to inspect Riley's body and the crimson splatters that stained the carpet. "Oh, dear, there seems to have been a brouhaha."

"Yes, I'm afraid there was. Please take care of Teddy."

I left Ziba with the slumbering child and followed the bloody trail through the corridor and the kitchen to the rear of the house.

A flurry had blanketed the courtyard with fresh snow. In the stillness, a dark figure left a scarlet footpath as he stumbled toward his carriage. I trailed after him, numb to the cold. Dr. Reeves slid to the ground just as a female voice called my name. "Delight, our Delight." I turned.

Abby, Clara, and Patsy jumped from a carriage, and Edgar limped after them. Abby called out to me. "Edgar sought us at the rooming house. He said his father had gone insane. We came—"

Her voice trailed when she saw Dr. Reeves lying on a snowy bed that turned a brighter shade of scarlet with each heartbeat. Edgar knelt and touched the wound.

"Who did this?"

"I did. Your father tried to kill me, Teddy as well. I had to defend myself and protect the child."

The stream of blood had slowed to a trickle, and Edgar cradled Dr. Reeves's head in his lap.

"Father, there's nothing to be done. The cut is too deep. Blink if you understand."

The doctor closed and opened his eyes.

"Father, you'll die."

He blinked once again. Edgar whispered to the dying man. "Father, please, blink if you ask for God's forgiveness."

Dr. Reeves gaped at his younger son, disgust on his face and then he died, his eyes open in defiance. Without warning, Edgar cried out, whooping with excitement.

"He's dead. I'm free! I'm free!"

My last memory was of Abby wrapping her arms around me and leading me toward Bram House. "It will be all right, Delight. Everything will be all right."

Chapter 25

Charade

Laudanum erased the days following the deaths. I finally emerged from my haze into a cologne-scented bedchamber. When the opiates dissipated, I had vague recollections of Abby, Clara, and Patsy keeping vigil over me.

I stumbled from the bed and made my way to the mirror. Who was the bedraggled gypsy staring back at me? Famished and in need of a bath, I prepared myself for the worst. I had killed two men and awaited my punishment. I remembered Lucy Stone's quote, "Today we are fined, imprisoned, and hanged without a jury trial by our peers."

Since women could not serve on juries, I would surely face twelve men who would avenge Dr. Reeves. Death by hanging was painful, but I prayed it would be quick.

I seized what strength I could and made my way to the kitchen. Bride stood at the stove, her back to me.

"Hello, Bride."

She turned and gasped at my appearance. "Oh, Miss Thorpe, you poor thing."

Hecuba meowed and rubbed against my legs. Thanks be to God, Riley had not touched the cat. I searched for Teddy and did not see him. Dear God, had that vile man murdered my little angel?

"Where is Teddy? Bride, please tell me, where is he?"

My tone appeared to startle her. "The little one is fine, miss. He's in the stable with my husband. The poor tyke keeps asking for you." She crossed herself. "Things are well. You'll be happy to hear my mam is better. Please, miss, excuse me for saying it, you're a fright."

Yes, of course, I must have looked like a mad woman. Since the Boston police would surely be calling on me, perhaps I should ready myself for my arrest. "A bath would be good, Bride. I should prepare for—later."

She gave me a confused look and nodded. "Yes, of course. I'll heat water for your bath. Will you eat first, miss?"

A breakfast cooked by Bride Greer might be the last decent meal I would ever have. She plopped down a feast of eggs and sausage, and I consumed it with great pleasure. After my bath, I donned a simple black frock, one I hoped would be appropriate for my arrest and trial. The jet buttons might be excessive for a murderess, but except for that small ornamentation, the gown would be perfect.

I moved to the dining room, the best place to await the authorities. The morning's edition of *The Boston Globe* lay on the monstrous dining table. Its front page featured a handsome engraving of Dr. Reeves with a caption that read, *Boston has lost its most favored son, Dr. Morris S. Reeves.*

Did I dare read it? Yes, of course I must.

The article stated that the entire city mourned the great man of medicine. The venerable mayor of Boston had personally called upon Dr. Reeves's two sons,

Charles and Edgar, as well as a family friend, the lovely Miss Abigail Wentworth, to offer his condolences. The obituary made no mention of the blood-curdling details of the doctor's demise at the hand of a scalpel-wielding lunatic. I read on.

The Globe mentioned Dr. Reeves's marriage into one of the great families of the city after his heroic service with the famed Massachusetts 32nd Volunteer Infantry in the war. The obituary went on to detail his assistance to the poor and needy, and his brilliant schooling of another generation of doctors at the Harvard Medical School.

The obituary ended with a reference to his tragic death and quoted the doctor's eldest son, Charles Clayton Reeves of the Harvard Medical School. *"Father died because he was a healer who always put the care of a sick patient above his own well-being."*

My head began to throb. I stopped reading and tried to collect my senses but to no avail.

"Father, devoted physician that he was, heard of a child in need. He left the comfort of our home to rush to the side of the poor tyke. In his haste, he drove his coupe with great speed, and it overturned in the newly fallen snow. He broke his neck in the accident. I thank the Lord that he died instantly. Mercifully, the child recovered. Can it be that the Almighty in His infinite wisdom chose to spare the tyke and bring His devoted son home?"

Dear God in Heaven, was everyone in Boston part of this deception? Perhaps Bride could enlighten me. Before I could ask, Ziba entered and rushed to me, arms open in an embrace. She wore a dark brown gown trimmed in black fur.

"My darling Delight, we've been so worried. I'm

sorry to abandon you, but Miss Wentworth has requested our presence at tea today. I'll convey your regrets. Please excuse me, I must get my cloak and bonnet."

She had turned to leave, but I stopped her with my words. "I want to join you for your tea with Miss Wentworth."

Ziba swiveled around, her forehead furrowed in vexation. "Delight, please, I must insist you stay here. One slip of the tongue, one misstep on your part will be the ruination of us all. Few know what happened that night. My darling girl, you should rest."

She addressed me in the same condescending tones that had angered me from my first night. It would not do.

"Rest? I've done nothing but rest for two days. Take me with you, Ziba. Don't leave me here. I won't spoil the ruse. After all, if I slip, I'll be the one dancing from the gallows."

Ziba's face reddened, and she paced the room, agitated. "You stubborn girl! Do you have any idea of what we did while you slept? Edgar and the girls dragged Dr. Reeve's body to the basement. To our great relief, Mr. Greer returned. He and Abby embalmed the monster while Edgar and the twins rolled Riley's vile carcass into a carpet. Edgar took it to Harvard for dissection. Thank the Lord that the new snow covered the blood."

I remembered the blood. Would it show after the spring thaw?

Ziba's tone sharpened. She whipped her head around in my direction and glared at me. "Delight, are you listening? The next morning, after Edgar told me what had happened, the girls and I cleansed the place of gore. Charles and another student signed the death certificate and lied to the authorities. All of us have sworn never to tell the truth to a living soul."

She stopped pacing, and her voice suddenly calmed. "We're all part of a conspiracy. One errant word will bring our ruin and inform the world of Dr. Reeve's misdeeds. Drusilla Wentworth believes Charles's account of his father's death, but if you stumble, you'll take us all down with you."

"Ziba, I shall go with you."

"No."

I felt blood come to my face. All the anger I had stifled for weeks rose to the surface. "I came to Bram House willing to work my fingers to the bone just for a home. How did you reward me? With generous servings of terror and duplicity. Do you think I regret my actions on that hideous night? I don't. I'd do it again gladly to protect you and Teddy, my only family. Now I see the world for what it truly is. Ziba, if you don't let me accompany you, I'll visit Miss Wentworth alone."

Ziba left the room without a word. When she returned, she wore a fine new bonnet of black velvet and ebony lace. She handed me my winter cloak and a fur-trimmed bonnet and walked away. "Very well. It's time for us to be off."

Chapter 26

Drusilla Wentworth

Wentworth House remained its heavy, oppressive self, still very much a museum, and the appropriate place to wake Dr. Reeve's body. When we arrived, mourners made their way toward the parlor where his corpse lay in state. A butler led us into Miss Wentworth's apartments and spared us the sight of the departed. We found our hostess playing the *grande dame,* while her devoted companions, Charles, Miss India Warren, and Edgar, danced in attendance.

Upon seeing me enter, Charles nearly choked on his tea. His face reddened, and he turned to Edgar as if questioning the wisdom of having me in the room.

I noted a marked change in Drusilla Wentworth's appearance. She'd coiffed her hair in the fashionable Titus cut with pale wisps artfully framing her face. Her exquisite black velvet *toilette* gave a glimpse of her milk-white bosom.

Ziba whispered, "I've never seen such a beautiful gown. It must have come from Worth's in Paris." Mourning truly became Drusilla Wentworth.

Miss Wentworth rose from her chaise and took Ziba's hand in greeting. "Madame Thorpe, thank you for coming to tea, it is wonderful to see you again." She turned her head in my direction, appraising me, her beautiful face revealing nothing.

"And this lovely young thing must be Miss Thorpe. We didn't speak on your last visit, but we'll remedy it today. Please, everyone, do sit."

For the next two hours, we smiled, simpered, and jested, consumed finger sandwiches, pastries, and endless cups of sugared tea. We chatted about the weather, the recent presidential election, the new fashions, and the theater. Finally, Miss Wentworth broached the subject Charles had hoped to avoid. "Before you arrived, I asked Charles how we can survive without his dear father."

Charles remained silent. Miss Wentworth filled my cup with the amber liquid. "More tea, Miss Thorpe? Please, may I call you by your given name? Delight isn't it? You must call me Cilla as my friends do. Two sugars? Madame Thorpe? Edgar? Charles?"

She poured cups for her guests, replaced the teapot, and paused to dab at a dry eye. "The city is reeling from the tragedy of poor Dr. Reeves's untimely death." I shifted in my chair, Edgar scrutinized his boots, Ziba adjusted her gloves, and Charles looked away.

Miss Wentworth continued speaking after the uncomfortable silence. "The dear man reposes downstairs. Your servant, Greer, brought him yesterday. Except for a bruise on his cheek, it is as if he were slumbering. All of Boston will come for the viewing."

No one said a word and a chipper Miss Wentworth ignored the silence. "Edgar has informed me that he and Charles have spared no expense on their father's entombment. It should be a funeral to remember, the grandest in the history of the city, replete with pipes and drums. Charles has engaged Trinity Church, and the good Reverend Phillips Brooks will give the eulogy."

She turned to Charles, her lips fixed in a determined pout. "May I suggest a team of black stallions with plumed headdresses and a glass hearse so the onlookers may admire the casket?"

Charles gave an unenthused nod. "Yes, of course, Cilla. A glass hearse will be beautiful indeed. The funeral cortege will travel from Trinity Church to Cambridge. Edgar and I briefly entertained the idea of burying Father in the Garden, but we decided Mount Auburn would be the place of his final repose. Isn't that so, Edgar?"

Edgar grunted his agreement.

Miss Wentworth rose from the chaise. "Wonderful, wonderful, I'm overjoyed you'll put your father away in style. Now, I hope you'll excuse me, for I wish to have a moment alone with Delight. I've purchased several new gowns from Paris that I wish to show her, and I know she'll be curious to see them. Please excuse us for a moment."

Ziba set her cup and saucer down. "Miss Wentworth, Cilla, our Delight is still recovering from a winter cold. Perhaps you might show her your French fashions another day."

Drusilla Wentworth stretched her beautiful mouth into a brittle smile.

"Dear Mrs. Thorpe, I believe I requested a word alone with your niece."

Ziba bowed her head in submission. Miss Wentworth took my arm, and we left the room.

****

I followed Miss Wentworth into her bedchamber, a frilly, lilac-scented affair, the walls swathed in blue silk.

Her maid had arranged yellow hothouse roses in crystal vases that sat atop a bureau and dressing table enameled in gentle tones of taupe. An immense wardrobe carved from the finest teak took up an entire wall.

Beautiful *toilets* lay across chairs and tables, alongside piles of boxes housing fashionable hats. She picked up a feathered bonnet. "It's from the House of Worth, the most fashionable *maison de création de mode* in Paris. I used to hide my purchases, but since Mama is no longer here, I dress to please myself."

"Miss Wentworth—"

She turned to me with another faux smile plastered across her face. "Dear Delight, I know we'll become fast friends. Once again, I must insist you call me Cilla." Miss Wentworth plopped one of the bonnets on her head with a giggle then turned to me, her face suddenly quite serious. "My dear, I have a most indelicate matter to discuss."

Her words were like a noose tightening around my neck. Could Drusilla Wentworth have discovered that Dr. Reeves died by my hand? I prayed the Savior would permit my farewells to Teddy and the Greers before the law transported me to the gallows. Had Charles betrayed me? No, it could not be. It was far too dangerous for him. Besides, she had asked me to call her Cilla. If she wished my destruction, why would she insist I address her with such intimacy?

"I received your letter, Delight, and I know what you wish to discuss."

In all the trouble of the last few days, I had forgotten about the letter. What did this elegant young woman know about body snatching?

Her grin brightened. She donned another bonnet and admired her image in a large mirror. "My dear girl, a few days after you arrived in Boston, Charlie informed me of his deep feelings for you."

I struggled to keep my composure despite her forced conviviality. "You must understand, dear girl, I grew up with the Reeves boys. Our parents hoped Charles and I would wed. I beg you, my dear, you must forget any claim you have to Charlie's affections."

"Do you love him?"

I had my answer when she averted her face.

"No. Unfortunately, I find the idea of wifely obligations odious. If you must know, dear Delight, I find the male member loathsome. Once, my inebriated cousin Freddy exposed himself to me, and I'll never recover from the sight!"

Cilla suddenly remembered herself and patted her eyes with a perfumed handkerchief. "Charlie is of a most amorous nature and has always made it clear he expects children. Please, don't think ill of me, but I detest babies. They're disagreeable and quite smelly. Unfortunately, Mother insisted I must marry Charlie or lose everything. Dr. Reeves's will made the same stipulation on his son. In any case, I don't intend to acquiesce to any man. Now that my mother is dead as is Dr. Reeves, Charlie and I have come to a decision. We will marry and have one child. Only then will I live a separate existence with my dear friend, India. My only request is for you to keep silent about his declaration of love to you. Will you?"

Her comments stunned me, and I could not speak. I nodded in agreement. With those few words, Cilla Wentworth lifted the weight of the world from my shoulders. I recalled Dr. Reeves referring to her as Mrs.

Wentworth's "*Sapphic daughter*." From my Greek studies, I remembered the poet, Sappho, had established a colony of young women on the isle of Lesbos. Was Cilla a poetess? Perhaps she would show me her work one day.

She took my hand in hers and opened her heart. "Since Mother's death, I've created a life for myself. After all, I'm eighteen now. Don't judge me too harshly, but the reason I buried her so quickly was I couldn't bear her presence, even in death. You may think me a monster, but I didn't love her."

So, everything about Cilla Wentworth was a sham. Her devotion to her mother was as counterfeit as her ardor for Charles. Still, I gave her hand a gentle squeeze.

"Cilla, your secrets are safe with me."

****

Dr. Reeves's burial occurred at noon on December 23, 1880. Edgar called out when I entered the courtyard with Bride and Teddy. "Delight, we're waiting. Please don't tarry."

I dressed in a black cashmere gown refashioned from one of Ziba's finer cast-offs. Ziba locked arms with an unsmiling Edgar who stood in front of the carriage, top hat in hand. He had come under the ministrations of his father's French valet and was now every inch the gentleman. Surely, he was comforted that the nightmare of the past was finally at an end.

I would soon take part in the funeral of the man I had killed and took no comfort when Edgar squeezed my hand. Before I could step into the carriage, childish laughter disturbed the quiet.

The brats raced down Browning Lane, screaming

their customary chant. "Worm's meat and maggot pie!" The scamps charged past, except for the little girl who took a tentative step into the courtyard and beckoned to Teddy.

"Come here, funny boy!" Teddy pulled away from Bride's and ran to her. "Hello, funny boy. My name is Pearl. Who are you?"

Teddy had never had a foray into the world of other children. He looked from Bride to Ziba to me and then extended his hand. "Theodore."

Pearl giggled as she took his hand. "Theodore? I don't like that name. I'll call you Billy. Come with me, Billy."

The two moppets scurried off into the Garden. Ziba moved to follow them, but I barred her way. "Leave them alone. Bride will watch after Teddy."

Bride dashed after the tykes, yelling as she ran. "You little villains. Come back here, or there won't be no gingerbread for you."

We took our places in the funeral carriage with Edgar sitting across from Ziba and me. The funeral was interminable as was the long trek to the Reeves mausoleum in Mount Auburn. There were pipers, testimonials, and mourners feigning grief.

At Charles's invitation, the young ladies of the embalming class attended and sat with us. We locked hands and watched as the youthful pallbearers carried his casket on their shoulders in the silent procession. I wondered if the young men's solemn faces hid their disappointment at not having his body for dissection.

The funeral ended, and finally, we were on our way back to Bram House. Ziba surveyed the carriage. "The services were as grand as those for a head of state." She gave Edgar a gentle pat on the knee. "I'm sure your father would be pleased."

Edgar flashed at her, his eyes brimming with tears. "Father wouldn't be pleased with his coffin on display before all of Boston. He would hate this vulgar cortege. He'd find it odious to rest in the family mausoleum with those he hated. It's his comeuppance for cajoling and bending everyone to his will, for his part in murder and deceit. He tried to avenge himself on those he despised and in doing so, nearly destroyed us all. It took poor Delight to put an end to his cruelty. I pray that God will forgive him. I can't."

The poor dear broke down and wept. Ziba and I watched him, both of us as sober as two judges.

****

An hour later, Edgar, Ziba, and I entered Bram House greeted by the laughter of my embalming sisters who had arrived before us. Abby bounced over to us and grabbed Ziba's hand. "Madame Thorpe, you must see the wondrous treats Mrs. Greer has baked for us."

Before Ziba headed to the kitchen, she turned back to Edgar. "This has been an eventful day. I hope you'll join us for supper." She glanced from Edgar to me and colored slightly. "Goodness, I smell pumpkin pie, my favorite. Excuse me."

Ziba looked back at us and then headed for the kitchen with a salacious giggle.

Edgar remained at my side. "Delight, I must speak before I lose all courage. Please, be honest with me. Is there the slightest chance that you might consider me?"

I placed my hand over his mouth. "After all that has transpired, we shouldn't speak of such things. We've just buried your father. I killed him, I—"

He removed my hand and took it in his. "You brought down a mad dog who would have ruined everything I hold dear. He destroyed my mother, and I never had a moment of affection for him. I love you, my darling."

When he took my face in his hands, I felt compelled to speak.

"I'm only seventeen as you are. Perhaps this might wait until we are older."

He seemed pleased I had not denied him outright. He dug into his pocket and pulled out a sprig of greenery covered with white berries. "Edgar, whatever is that?"

He moved closer and held the twigs over my head. "It's mistletoe. I've been carrying it these two days in hopes of seeing you alone."

I did not avert my face. "Oh, yes, I've heard about mistletoe. It's not a good plant. It is a parasite; however, I've heard it has interesting uses during Christmastide though I've never—"

Before I finished speaking, Edgar pulled me to him and kissed me. His lips were soft, and he smelled of peppermint lozenges. "Delight, I beg of you, is there a chance that one day you might find me worthy?" How could he ask such a thing? I had killed his father.

I looked deep into his eyes and saw my answer. He loved me.

"Edgar, I'll only say that patience is the virtue I most admire."

His smile outshone the sun. We kissed again.

****

The long day finally ended. Despite the circumstances, supper was most jolly. Mr. Greer joined us at our table, and the girls spoke of upcoming

Christmas festivities in Boston. The emerald ring flashed from Ziba's finger. Like me, she agreed we should be practical. A beaming Abby took a sip of eggnog and tittered. "For once, we'll have a Yuletide to remember."

After the darkness of the day, I finally understood why Ziba used humor to lighten the mood. I decided to give it a try. "Everyone, please listen. I have a joke to share. What is the difference between a tube and a foolish Dutchman?" They stared at me with rapt attention. "One is a hollow cylinder, and the other is a silly Hollander."

Raucous laughter erupted throughout the room. I had made people forget the darkness of the past, if only for a moment, and felt quite grand about it. Afterward, Ziba took to her bed, and Edgar and the girls departed. I sat alone in my chamber reflecting on my time in Boston. My journal sat on the étagère wrapped in brown paper.

December 23, 1880

The Good Hope Inn

Rachel's Pride, Massachusetts

Miss Charity Yates

Dearest Gentle Friend,

I am entrusting my diary into your hands. It is a testament to the events of the recent past, a "souvenir" as the French call it, a remembrance of that most horrible time. You of course have your own memories of the sad autumn of 1880 when we both suffered so greatly. I lost everything dear to me in those torturous days, and the events detailed in this slim volume have transformed me into the pitiful creature I am now. I pray that in reading these pages you will come to better understand my actions and judge me with a benevolent heart. Regretfully, what has passed cannot be undone.

So you can better fathom my unhappy tale, I am also sharing pages I purloined from Ziba's diary. She has since burned her journals and will never discover my thievery. Her writing will surely shock you, but it will help understand her motives. Ziba and I have a most amiable relationship, but there is a gulf that will take time to bridge. In all likelihood, beloved friend, the two of us will go to our graves sheltering these dreadful secrets. It is my cross and pains me more than I can say, but even more excruciating is the agony we all share because of him.

Dear comrade, please read all that I have placed in your care, the details of which are of a most shocking nature. Unfortunately, everything written is true. After you have pored over these pages, I beg you, burn them immediately. They are for your eyes only and cannot be consigned into the hands of others.

Know, gentle friend, that you are the only person on this earth to whom I can reveal this horror in its entirety. I regret burdening you, but if this tale remains secreted in my heart and languishes there, if it is not shared with another living soul, I shall wither away and die. I ask only that you try to make sense of the transgressions of your poor friend.

Delight

I placed the letter in an envelope and would mail it along with the journal after the holidays. Until I arrived in Boston, I had never caused injury to anyone and lived a life of charity and caring for others. It seemed my good deeds had been for naught. I had killed two men. Despite their evil, I prayed for their eternal salvation. In the darkness of my chamber, I thought of my friends and family, old and new. I gazed at the images of my parents and realized the truth. Those who loved me were my ghosts, protective spirits who had kept me from an entanglement with Charles. Amidst the pain and horror, I had also found love with Edgar and sisterhood with the embalming girls. Boston would be my home and preparing the bodies of those who had passed on, my profession. Although we readied the dead for eternal rest, our true purpose was to succor the living.

A word about the author...

Lee Rene is a jazz-loving author of Young Adult and New Adult novels. She had the good fortune of being born in one the most diverse cities in the world, sun-kissed Los Angeles. The City of the Angels is more than just palm trees, toned bodies, movie stars, and beaches, it's a fusion of people, languages, and cultures. In her past literary life, Lee worked as a lifestyle writer for magazines in Los Angeles, San Francisco, New York, and Vancouver as well as entertainment journalist and movie reviewer in print, online, and on radio in the Los Angeles area. She is a student of American history, and her works are often set in the past. The Boston Embalming Girls is the product of years of researching the origins of the funeral industry and is a provocative look at a little-known part of American history.

Thank you for purchasing
this publication of The Wild Rose Press, Inc.

For questions or more information
contact us at
info@thewildrosepress.com.

The Wild Rose Press, Inc.
www.thewildrosepress.com

Milton Keynes UK
Ingram Content Group UK Ltd.
UKHW020738071024
449371UK00014B/935

9 781509 255733